HIDING IN THE DARK

An Ellie Lynn Moore Mystery

Sava Mathou

Fulton Books, Inc.
Meadville, PA

Published by Fulton Books 2020

ISBN 978-1-64654-029-7 (paperback)
ISBN 978-1-64654-030-3 (digital)

Printed in the United States of America

This book is dedicated to Kym Rapier (friend/family), Ann Nord (mother), Tracy Schultz (sister), Danielle Baranski (sister), Rochelle Nord (sister), Alissa Runsat (sister/Bestie/fabulous), Lily Yamamoto (superstar), Elise Buffalo (fellow goddess), Samantha (Binnie) Talks Different (friend/sister/spooner), Janet LeDuc (Fave Aunt), Gina O'Connell (fellow Cher fan/friend), Rebecca Webber-Pollock (friend/makes me laugh), Chick Kennedy (bingo buddy/sister), Debbie Nichols (big heart), Gisele Noble-Lamper (smart cookie), April Mitzie Webber (sassy pants), Melissa Brune' (amazing inside and out), Phyllis Townsend-McCuller (awesome), Sherry Gigous (extraordinary writer), Christine Rodgers (a great person), Vernisha Coleman (just love her), Terri Hamilton (such kindness), and Kendra Buffalo (sister from another mister).

You are some of the strongest and bravest women, that I am so proud to know. I love you all! Thank you!

Thank you to my son's, Chad and Alex Gibbons (twin son's.) I am proud to say that I am your dad and you are my son's. I love you both so much! You have turned into amazing young men!

Thank you to my partner, David Donaldson. I appreciate your love and support. Thank you!

Sava

PROLOGUE

At fifty-five, Ellie needed some adventure. This is the story of a vibrant and tough Montana-bred woman who wanted to shake up her life.

Ms. Ellie had always been a lady of leisure. However, in her waning years, she longed for some adventure. She was now fifty-five years old, and she wanted some excitement in her life. Her children were grown and had moved onto their own lives. They had little time in their busy lives to get home and visit their lonely old mother. She didn't blame or hold a grudge against them. It was only natural they want to build a career and start families of their own. Besides, they came home for every holiday. She got to be surrounded by their love, and in many ways, she felt blessed. If she told them she was lonely, they would drop what they doing and head right home to her side. Ms. Ellie didn't feel right, asking them to drop what they were doing just because she was lonely. She would find a new path in her life to keep her busy. Besides, she had been planning a new career for a while.

Janet, her daughter, was now living in Missoula with her family. She had graduated from the University of Montana–Missoula with a degree in law and was now a successful lawyer. Just like her father, her job kept her quite busy, and she thrived on it. Her husband, Dave, was also a lawyer who moved to Montana from somewhere on the East Coast. Ellie couldn't remember exactly where as Dave never spoke about his family very much. He had had a falling out with his father some years ago and decided to move West to escape the family turmoil. He made Janet very happy and was a good man. It brought a thoughtful smile to her lips, knowing that her daughter was happy and building a life with Dave. Now if she would just have some grandchildren, then all would be right in the world.

John Jr. also had gone into law and had moved to Billings shortly after law school. He had been recruited by a local oil and gas company right out of law school. He now handled the real estate aspects on the firm's oil and gas leases. He seemed to be doing well but didn't talk much about work or his life to his mother. She never had a doubt that John Jr. didn't love her as his mother, but he had always been quiet. He wasn't secretive about his work or life. It was just in his nature not to talk much.

John Jr. always said that he spoke so much for a living that when it came to his private life that he just didn't have much say. Ellie worried about him because she never quite knew what was happening in his life. He always told her what was going on if she asked. However, as he got older, she began to feel like she was intruding.

Ms. Ellie began to think of her husband. He had passed on a few years back. The passing left her with a grief that she thought she would never be able to work through. Over time, the pain lessened, but the longing had always remained. John had always been a supportive and loving husband. When so many of her friend's husbands were off, cheating with their secretaries or mistresses. John had always remained faithful.

He was a good man, she thought. A blush rising her in cheeks.

Never once during their thirty-five years of marriage had he even given her an inkling that he looked at another woman. His friends would tease him that the sun rose and set on his wife. As far as John Sr. was concerned, that was exactly right. John would see the problems and situations that arose among his friends for the infidelities they had. It was a life that he wanted no part of in this world. Ellie had been everything he wanted in a wife, partner, and friend.

They had been childhood sweethearts. Both families encouraged the match from early on. It brokered two powerful Montana families together. Everyone was happy at their union although they needed no encouragement from family or friends. They had always known that that they loved one another and that there would never be anyone else.

They had lived the perfect life. She knew she was very fortunate to have been given such a life. She looked back with fulfillment and happiness.

Her husband's sudden death came as a surprise and left her with a hole in her soul. She had tried to fill the void with volunteer work and social functions. All these things still left her feeling as though something was missing. She began to realize that she had never really done anything for and completely just for her. Ellie never regretted her life with John and wouldn't change a thing. At this stage in her life, she began to realize she wanted something more. She wanted something that was going to give her excitement and adventure. She knew that she would never love again. John had been all the man she needed and doubted that there would ever be another. Ellie counted herself lucky to have found such a love.

CHAPTER ONE

"Become a private eye," the advertisement read.

Ellie lay on the bed and daydreamed of the adventures she could have. Her children would probably want to have her committed if they knew she wanted this. This time, they would know she had flipped her lid. It had been very difficult when John Sr. died and left her alone. She fought so hard to escape the hole she was sinking in after his death. John Jr. had wanted to have a live-in nurse brought into her home to keep her company. Ellie railed against this idea. She was in the prime of her life, and she certainly didn't need looking after by some nurse. Jr. had had no malice in his heart when he brought up the idea. He had simply been worried about his mother.

Over the many months after John Sr.'s death, Ellie had lost weight and had become rather gaunt. She had not even begun to recognize her own self in the mirror. It was no wonder her kids were worried. Truth be told. Ellie was a bit worried herself. Life had thrown her a curve ball, and she had no idea what to do next.

Ellie loved murder mysteries. Her personal library was filled with all the latest volumes from the newest authors. Books by the Volume had always been her home away from home. Sometimes, she giggled to herself because she had probably put Sue and Chuck's kids through college. They were the owners of the bookstore and always kept their eyes out for the newest and latest books to thrill Ellie's imagination.

In fact, Sue and Chuck had become instrumental in Ellie finding something new in her life to fill her time. They worried about her spending so much time alone up in that big ole house. Their relationship had started out years ago as customer and business owner and had developed into a lifelong friendship. Their love of literature solidified their relationship. It was with their encouragement that Ellie began to rejoin the land of the living. Sue continued to bring over a new book on each visit. Soon Ellie's night table had begun to fill with unread books.

Ellie no longer wanted to read the type of books she loved. All these people in those pages were having such grand adventures, and here she is, lying in bed. Growing old and withered before her own eyes, she wanted her own adventures. She got up from the bed and pushed the growing pile of books to the floor. It was not out of anger but more out of a new self that she would begin to create. Deciding that she was not going to let life defeat her now, Ms. Ellie Lynn Moore would be someone in her own right. Even if she failed doing it, at least she would know that she had tried.

Bes*ides, what fifty-five-year-old woman would become a private detective without having a few screws loose?* she thought. The thought brought her mind, swimming back to her husband. John Sr. had told her more than once, "Ellie, I think you were a gumshoe in your past life!"

Ellie would turn red and reply, "Oh, John. Don't be ridiculous. Me? A gumshoe? Though the thought of it does sound thrilling."

Standing in her room, she began to really look at herself in the mirror. For the first time in a while, Ellie caught just the twinkle in her own eyes. She began to see the old Ellie peek out from beneath the surface. Looking herself over, there were a few sags and wrinkles, showing in her face. But for a fifty-five-year-old woman, Ellie thought she had held up well over the years. Realizing that she was a grandmother, she smiled. What else was she supposed to look like?

It was decided right then and there, in front of the mirror, that she would become a private eye.

Now, how exactly did one do that?

Where is that darn advertisement? Ellie's mind raced.

Pushing aside the books that were now piled on the floor, she grasped a hold of the paper with a renewed vigor for life. Whipping through the pages of the circular paper, her eyes scanned the pages for the advertisement. Finding it near the back of the paper, a huge sigh of relief escaped her. It surprised her. She had sounded like she had just found her lost diamond, and it was a way she had.

Reading over the advertisement, self-doubt began to rise with in her. Silently, she sat on the edge of the bed. The paper clasped within her fists. She hit the paper against her legs with a slap. Quickly, she dialed the 800 number. Her fingers trembled as she punched in the numbers. Inside, she felt like a mischievous little girl, stealing the first warm cookie from the batch just out of the oven.

In her ear, she could hear the ring in the ear piece. Holding the phone to her head, sweat began to bead on her forehead. Her cheeks filled with blood and took on a slight blush. Ellie's heart began to pound with in her chest.

"Hello. Thank you for calling Price Private Detective School. We are either away from the phone, or out in the field. Please leave a detailed message after the beep."

Beep. A shrill whistle of a beep sounded.

"Hello," she instinctively said.

"Yes. Hello. This is Ellie Moore, calling regarding the advertisement you have listed in our local circular paper. Please give me a call back at (406) 555-1291. I am calling about becoming a private detective and the school you run."

Click.

Quickly, she had hung up the phone, then grabbed the receiver and base and hugged it to her chest. Her heart was racing. Sweat was now covering her forehead and her under arms. She felt like she was already on a secret mission for someone. This time, it was for herself, and she let out a long sigh. The tenseness from her shoulders began to slip away.

Suddenly, the phone rang in her hands, frightening her. She almost whipped the darn thing over the bed. Ellie started to laugh as she answered. *Get a grip, woman*, she thought.

"Hello!" she answered with a huge grin on her face.

"Ellie, is that you?"

"Yes. It's me. Is that you, Sue?"

"Why do you sound so out of breath? Is everything all right? Do I need to come over?"

Always ready to send out the troops, she thought of Sue.

"No, no. I am fine. The phone just startled me for a moment. Guess my mind was off on another planet there for a moment." Ellie had to stifle a laugh before she got a bad case of the church giggles. You know the church giggles? This is where you laugh and just can't stop even though you know you should.

Exasperated, Sue said, "Now, you sound like you're on the verge of laughter? What is going on over there? What is going on with you, woman? Did I catch you with your hand in the cookie jar?"

Smiling, Ellie replied, "You might as well have. I was just taken by surprise. That is all. What is up?"

"I have got some of those books you ordered awhile back. Thought you might like to come by and pick them up? Besides, Chuck is out on some errands, and it's a slow day. Thought you might like a cup of coffee?"

"I don't think I will be needing those books any longer, but I do have some new books I would like to look into. How does a half hour sound?"

"Sounds good, but what are you up to? I know that tone." Sue listened to her friend in the phone with a new eagerness.

Nervously, she said, "Let's talk over coffee. I want to bounce a couple of ideas off you and see what you think of something I may be doing in the very near future."

"Okay. Half hour?"

"Half hour. See you then!"

Hanging up the phone, Ellie headed to the restroom to freshen up. Again, she was surprised by the face in the mirror. Smiling, she looked at herself and tried to think of what was different. She had just made a phone call and talked to Susan. Yet there it was, plain as day, written all over her face.

That's it!

A sparkle!

Ellie saw the sparkle of life back in her eyes. It surprised her because she honestly hadn't realized it was gone. No wonder her friends were so worried about her. She would have to call up the kids and reassure them that she was coming around and get them to come down for a visit. Maybe then, John Jr. would see she didn't need a live-in nurse. Still, she must have caused them some worry. If a bathroom mirror could be so truthful to her own self, then what must have her poor kids and friends thought? A phrase popped into her head, making her blush, *Time to grab the bull by the horns!* With that phrase stuck in her mind, Ellie squared her shoulders and smiled at herself in the mirror.

Driving over to Sue and Chuck's store, Books by the Volume, Ellie found herself, having to slow the car down. The mph dial was well over the legal limit. She was happy again. Summer had come to Helena, and she hadn't quite realized it. Now with the windows down, she felt the wind on her hair and skin and enjoyed driving a little faster than normal. She made good time, zipping up North Montana Avenue, turning right onto Cedar Street and heading toward Last Chance Gulch. Soon, Books by the Volume came into view on Last Chance Gulch.

As she parallel parked on Last Chance Gulch, it still amazed Ellie that people found gold, washing into the street after a good rain. Most tourists would never look to their feet during a rain but head for the nearest shelter, missing the chance to find a real piece of Montana gold and Montana history located just at their feet. Montana riches are hidden beneath their toes.

Across the street from her stood Books by the Volume. She saw Sue, standing on the old library ladder in the window, putting more new volumes on the upper shelves. Opening her car door, Ellie suddenly felt butterflies in her stomach. She was about to tell her best friend that this suburban housewife wanted to become a private detective. Ellie began to imagine the spirited calls to the nuthouse in Warm Springs. Whispered conversations in the background that Ellie Lynn Moore had finally lost her mind and gone around the bend. Ellie knew she was being a bit foolish in her new adventure, but it was something she was determined to do.

Taking a deep breath, she exhaled slowly and pushed herself up from the front seat of the car. It was now or never. She raced between cars and crossed the street. After all, she had only made a call. It wasn't like she had signed up for the course yet. She would tell Sue and gauge her reaction. Ellie hoped her friend wouldn't break down in front of her in hysterical laughter.

Grasping the handle on the front door of the bookstore. She felt as though her legs were going to give way and buckle at any moment. Now, she wished she hadn't told Sue to put bells on the front door to let her know when people arrived in the store. The bells signaled her entrance. Now Ellie wished she was invisible. Darn bells!

Sue called from the ladder, "Hey, hun. Be right with you in a minute. Help yourself to some coffee. Just have a couple more books to be put up."

"Okay!" was all she could muster.

Ellie made her way quickly to the back of the store and the fresh coffee. Now she wanted to avoid the coming conversation for as long as possible. Pouring herself a cup of coffee, she noticed her hands trembling.

Suddenly, a hand was on her shoulder. Jumping, she threw the coffee and dropped the coffee pot. It was only Sue. Ellie turned around to see Sue, staring at her with her mouth agape. Trembling, Ellie grabbed a hand full of napkins and began cleaning up the spilled coffee and broken glass without a word.

On her hands and knees, trembling and trying not to make eye contact with her best friend, Ellie's emotions suddenly drew to the surface.

Suddenly, Ellie began to cry.

Climbing to her feet, Ellie moved to the leather reading sofa and dropped her body into the couch. Head in her hands, Ellie began to cry for her husband, herself, her children, and their family. It suddenly dawned on her that she hadn't really cried since John Sr. died, and now, it was all coming out in a big blubbery mess. This wasn't supposed to happen now. She had come to the bookstore to tell her friend that she had finally pulled herself up by the boot straps and gotten her life back in order. This was not helping her look like she had gotten her life together again.

Sue let her friend cry. It was about time that she let loose all that hurt and anger over losing her husband. Instinctively, Sue knew why Ellie was crying. Her and her husband, Chuck, had been worried for a long time over their dear friend. Sometimes Ellie tried to put up a brave front for everyone else and wouldn't give herself the time to heal and recover. It was good now to see her friend, getting out the feelings that she had been holding inside for far too long. Frankly, it relieved Sue to know that her friend was finally touching on the feelings that she had bottled deep inside.

Quietly, Sue moved to the front door of the store and locked it. Grabbing the closed sign and putting it in the door, she drew the curtains to give her and Ellie privacy to be alone and talk. Something had been brewing in Ellie for the last week or two, and Sue knew it would come out sooner or later. It would just take some time for Ellie to work through, and when she was ready, she would come to Sue with her thoughts and want to talk. Looking over at her friend. Sue sat amazed that they had developed such a lasting rich friendship. She had grown to love Ellie like family and no longer thought of her as a customer. Ellie was more like a beloved member of Sue and Chuck's family.

When Ellie had first come into their new store many years ago, Sue saw a woman who was obviously wealthy and carried herself with such dignity and grace. The thought brought a tear to Susan's eye. Sue had been nervous to approach the woman in her store. Sue was a simple Montana farm girl and was immediately intimidated by the woman and her appearance. The thought now brought a smile to her face. Sue couldn't have been more wrong about Ellie. As soon as Ellie asked her about a book she was wanting, Sue had felt a toughness and a warmth from this woman. They had been friends ever since.

Sue moved back over to the sofa and put her arm around Ellie. With her other hand, she reached up and pulled Ellie's head softly to her shoulder. Remaining in their tender embrace for many minutes, Ellie cried out her loss in the protective touch of her friend. It was a moment that could only be shared by two old friends. Family.

Whispering, Sue rocked Ellie and said, "*Shh* now. It's all right. Let it all out. This has been coming for a while now. *Shh*. There now. It's all right. You just take your time and cry it all out."

*****

Driving back home, Ellie thought she had temporarily lost her mind. She had begun to blurt out everything to Sue. Sue never said a word but just sat back on the couch and listened. She didn't know if Sue was too shocked to say anything, or was simply being a friend and taking it all in. When her outburst of emotion was over, Sue had sat back, thinking with her chin in her hand. Ellie knew this was never a good sign. Sue usually only did this when she was powering up to let someone have it with both barrels. Instead, she heard this.

"Well, woman, it's about time you get off your duff and stop feeling sorry for yourself. I have been wanting to kick you in the butt for holding everything in all this time. But I should know by now that this is typical Ellie. Just waiting to spill over before picking up the pieces to move on. Now for this private detective business. If this is what you want to do, then I am all for it. Really. It doesn't surprise me none. You have had your head in those dime store novels for years. God knows that if anyone is going to do this, then it's you. You're gonna have one heck of time explaining this one to the kids. Although that's a conversation that I would love to hear, if only to be a fly on the wall."

Ellie could see the glazed look in Sue's eyes as she dazed off with a rueful smile at thought of their conversation.

Heck, Ellie had to laugh too. If her kids thought she was incompetent before, then they would now have some fuel for the fire.

Opening the door to her home, Ellie began to feel a course of loneliness seep in. Before it could grab hold, the phone's ring had snapped her out of it. She dashed across the foyer to answer the hall phone.

Out of breath, she answered, "Moore residence."

"May I speak with Mrs. Moore, please?"

"This is Mrs. Moore. How may I help you?"

"This is Dylan from the Price Private Detective School, returning your call."

*****

Ellie had stayed in Missoula for the six weeks of schooling it took to get her private detective license with the State of Montana. She had stayed with her daughter Janet and her husband while going to school.

It had been one heck of a conversation, telling the kids about the new adventure in her life. Janet and Dave had sat stone faced and closed mouth as she told them about her schooling that would begin in the morning. John Jr. had silently waited for his mother to finish her speech before diving into a million questions over speaker phone. It was the grand inquisition being performed on her by loved ones. She knew this was a battle she would have to face. It was a battle she must win to show her loved ones that she had regained her life and was moving on.

She had been impressed by the kids. After what seemed like hours and hundreds of questions later, they knew their mother had made up her mind. They didn't have to like it, but they were going to respect her wishes.

For now.

However, one hint of danger, and she knew they would come storming in hell or high water because nothing was going to happen to their mother. She briefly wept at their courage and sincerity and love for her. Then she laid down some of her own ground rules.

"First and foremost, I am your mother, and I love you all for giving me the best children a mother could ask for in life. Second, I am a grown and capable woman, and I have thought about this for many years. This is not a spur-of-the-moment decision, nor is it one that I have given little worry too. I know the danger and boredom this type of work entails. However, I need to move on with my life.

"It's been very difficult for me since your father passed away. It's been hard on all of us. I need a new direction, one that makes me want to get out of bed in the morning. All my life, I supported my husband's career. Then as a mother, I joyfully took on the role of a parent. I wouldn't trade those years for anything. They made me very happy and fulfilled. Now at this time in my life, I want to do something daring and outrageous and completely for me. I know you love me and want what is best for me. I just want your love and support while I do something for me that will make me happy and want to live again."

There was a round of murmurs.

Finally, John Jr. spoke up. "I must admit that the thought of you out in the middle of the night, tracking down God knows who scares me to death. I know once you have made up your mind that there is no changing it. So with a bit of unease, I support you. Scared for you, but I support you."

"We do too. My mom a private eye?" Janet said in more of statement of wonder.

CHAPTER TWO

Ellie decided to rent an office down town close to Books by the Volume rather than work out of her home. She wanted a place to go to every day, and this would make her get up and get moving. Plus that big old house could be a bit lonely at times. This way, she was close to Chuck and Sue and could pop in for coffee runs and some downtime visits. Also, it put her downtown closer to the action of where she needed to be. She wouldn't have to run all the way in from the North Hill area where her home was located. She would be close to the jail, courthouse, library, DMV, and any other placed that she needed to do research for a case.

The office she rented was a basement floor two room office with its own bathroom. The tiles in the ceiling were dull with age and had collected a few water spots over the years. The walls were painted a dull gray, and at first glance, it was dismal to look at. Ellie saw freshly painted walls and ceiling and a new desk near the basement office window where she could see right out onto Last Chance Gulch.

She loved the idea of being able to watch the world pass by from her hidden cubby hole. It already gave her a sense of excitement of the forbidden, looking into people lives as they passed by, the people not knowing that they were being watched from beyond their line of sight.

She saw bookshelves in the far corner for her reference library and files. In the center of the room, she would place a sofa and some comfortable chairs for research and meeting with new clients.

In the back room, she would fix up as a make-shift mini apartment. This way, if she was working late on a case, she could catch up on needed sleep and not have to drive all the way out into the valley to her home. Plus it would be a great place for cat naps on a slow day.

Over the next couple of weeks, Chuck and Sue helped clean the place up and got it ready for business. Janet even drove up from Missoula to do some furniture shopping with her. Ellie thought Janet's motives were more to check up on her and see firsthand where she would be working.

Ellie and Sue got the walls painted. Fresh curtains hung. Office plants to green the place up a bit. Ellie thought she went a bit over the top, buying the big executive desk at a real estate auction. Looking at the desk, she thought it gave the room presence and added a masculine touch to all the feminine decor. She had seen the desk in the paper and thought it would be perfect to add a touch of authenticity to the place. Its dark paneled wood and gilded leather top anchored the room. The moving men had a heck of time, getting it down the stairs and through the door. Now she sat back in her overstuffed desk chair and was quite proud of the new surroundings.

The walls were freshly painted in an earth tone that Ellie felt would sooth and ground her clients. The ceiling painted a fresh crisp white gave the ceiling some height and made the basement office less claustrophobic.

The couch and chairs were a plush maroon-red leather that she got down and the local furniture store. They were a bit overstuffed but still had graceful lines. They complimented the desk and softened it a bit.

She brought down some of the old bookshelves out of John Sr.'s library that were no longer being used. It was nice, having a bit of John in the room. She could see John, looking down from heaven with his arms crossed and a big smile on his face. He would be proud, and the shelves added a touch of dignity and class to the room.

Ellie had filled the shelves with every kind of book from skip tracing to picking a lock. Sue and Chuck had to be happy at the number of books she had ordered for the office. It was probably a bit too much, but she wanted to be prepared. Every night, she took a different book home and skimmed through and read a little. When her first client walked through the door, she would be prepared.

Tomorrow, her sign would arrive. She had picked out an oval-shaped sign with a white background and green-and-gold lettering.

She wanted to the sign to stand out. She had the sign company write out Moore Detective Agency with her new office number listed below. She kept it simple and did not want to overcrowd the sign.

Ellie also placed ads in the local newspaper, the Independent Record, and the local circular, the Mini Nickel. These ads made it feel all the more real for Ellie. She would have to wait a couple weeks for the new phone books and yellow pages to come out to see the ad she had placed in there.

After the sign went up, and the ads ran, she would be open for business.

The first week, the only time the phone rang it was from Sue or one of the kids. Her brain began to run over scenarios of what her first case may be like. It was starting to drive her a bit nuts, sitting in the office all day, waiting for the phone to ring. Ellie decided to run down to Books by the Volume for a coffee run. She needed a break from the office.

Sue looked up from the cash register as Ellie came through the door and said, "So how is the life of the private detective?"

"Let's just say that if I stare at that phone any longer, it's going to spontaneously combust right there on my desk!"

"That bad, huh?"

"No, not bad. I am just wondering if that phone is ever going to ring. I think I just have a case of the first-case jitters, not knowing what to expect and all." A bit of blues, coming out in her voice.

Sue knew that voice. "I think a nice raspberry mocha decaf latte is in order. Nothing like a little sugar and a heap of chocolate to chase the doldrums away."

"Sounds good. Could you throw a shot of whiskey in there too?" Ellie said half joking and half serious.

Sue arched her eyebrows and gave her friend a rueful smile. Much surprised because Ellie rarely, if ever, drank anything harder than her occasional glass of wine. Instead of liquor, she added extra raspberry and extra chocolate. At least she would get a nice sugar buzz.

*****

Getting back to her office, Ellie's heart began to beat faster as she saw the red light, flashing on her phone on the desk. Someone had a left a message while she was out! It was probably just her daughter or son, but you never know. She sat down in her desk chair and took a deep breath and exhaled slowly, releasing some of the built up tension in her shoulders. Slowly, she extended her arm until her finger was just over the play button. Trembling, her finger pressed play.

A man's voice sounded on the machine.

"This is Bill Wallace over in Wolf Creek. I saw your ad in the Independent Record. I would like to sit down and talk with you about the disappearance of my daughter, Shelby, last month. Please give me a call at 406-555-1298 to set up an appointment."

"A real call. A real live person just asked me to help him find his daughter!" Her mind was racing. If she had been twenty years younger, Ellie would have jumped up and done some cartwheels across a lawn!

Ellie seemed to remember seeing something on the news about a local girl gone missing, but she couldn't bring up the circumstances of what had happened.

Quickly, she booted up her new computer and brought the Independent Records web page and started looking for an article on the Shelby Wallace. Typing the girl's name into the search bar brought up the article quickly.

It read:

> Local Girl Gone Missing, Foul Play Suspected
> Wolf Creek. The local police reported that Shelby Wallace had not returned home Friday night after going to a party with some of her friends. Her abandoned vehicle was found parked along Little Wolf Creek Road just outside Wolf Creek. The keys were still in the ignition, and her purse was lying on the passenger seat.
> A search was done of the local area. Tracking dogs were brought in and searched the area with no luck.

Her parents, Jane and Bill Wallace, were unavailable for comment at press time.

Anyone with any news or tips is asked to contact the Lewis and Clark County Sheriff's office, or can leave a message on the Crime Stoppers hotline.

This didn't give much for Jane to go on. She picked up the phone and dialed the number that Mr. Wallace had left on the answering machine. On the third ring, a voice answered the phone.

"Bill Wallace here."

"Mr. Wallace, this is Ellie Moor, calling from the Moore Detective Agency. You called earlier to talk about your daughter that is missing." Ellie was hoping her voice wouldn't crack, or sound nervous over the phone.

"Yes. I am in Helena. Do you have time to meet today?" An urgency was in his voice.

"Let me just check my book." Empty pages, staring at her. She didn't want to seem too eager. "How about one o'clock?"

Mr. Wallace agreed quickly, and Ellie gave him directions to the office. It was 12:30 p.m. now, and he would be here in a half hour. Ellie quickly threw out the old coffee and brewed a fresh batch. She set out a tray of mugs and some cookies on the coffee table next to the sofa. Walking quickly to the bathroom, she splashed some cold water on her face and fixed her mussed hair. Straightening her blouse, she thought, *This is it.*

A real case.

Mr. Wallace arrived early at ten to one. Ellie got up from behind her desk and welcomed the man and shook his hand. She looked at the man's face that was ashen in color and filled with worry. Dark circles were forming under his eyes, and she knew that sleep had not been coming easy to this man. Ellie had the same look after her husband had died, and she recognized the pain in his eyes right off. Instantly, she felt a connection to the man, leading him over to the sofa and offering him coffee.

With pleasantries aside, she picked up her pad of paper and pen off the coffee table.

"What can I do for you, Mr. Wallace?" She hoped her voice didn't betray her the fear she was feeling and let him know that she was scared to death.

"Bill. Please call me Bill." His voice was giving way to a slight crack in his armor.

"All right. Bill." She smiled. "What can I do for you?"

"As I said on the phone, my daughter went missing last month. Her car was found near our home, and we want to find our daughter." Sadness and anger, filling his voice.

"Tell me a little about your daughter," she said.

"Shelby would be nineteen this coming month. I mean, she will be nineteen this coming month."

Trying to recover from talking about her in the past tense, tears began to fill his eyes. Ellie handed him a tissue while letting him regain his composure. Ellie sat patiently, waiting for him to continue.

"Shelby is 5'4", 120 pounds, brown hair, brown eyes, and is petite in her build. Here is a picture that I brought of her. It was her senior portrait that she took when she graduated, but she still looks quite the same."

"You have a beautiful daughter, Mr. Wallace. I mean Bill." Looking at the picture, Ellie began to see the family resemblance. "Tell me about the events of that night and the last time you saw her."

"That evening, Shelby was getting ready for a night out with some friends of hers from school. She had asked me if I would lend her a few dollars for gas money. You know how kids are, always with the handout." His attempt at humor lost. "I spoke with her in the living room of our home. I gave her a twenty for gas. Told her to be careful, and to call if she needed a ride. We didn't want her drinking and driving and always told her call in she got herself in a spot."

"Did she happen to mention where she would be going and with who?"

"She never said, but I assumed it was with her girlfriends. She always hung with Stacy Ketchum and Lynn Heart. They had all been childhood friends and have remained close." Bill rattled off their phone numbers, and their addresses.

"Do you have any idea where they might have gone that evening?"

"My wife spoke with Stacy and Lynn. They told her that they went down to the ball field at the school in Wolf Creek. Had a few beers with their friends. Then Shelby dropped them off and said she was headed home. Her car was found about an hour after dropping them off at home. It was parked on Little Wolf Creek Road by the new bridge. The keys were still in the ignition, and her purse was lying on the front passenger seat. Nothing was taken from the car or her purse as far as we could tell."

"What did the police say about investigating the case?" She would have to get that report.

"They said there were no signs of foul play. They brought in the bloodhounds and did a search of the area and came up with nothing. Her friend's stories all confirmed what I told you already. The police think she may have run off with a man and told us that we will probably get a call from her any day now. If that's the case, then why would she not take her purse and just leave the car in the middle of the road? None of this makes sense."

"Was she involved with any men that you know?" Bill looked up at Ellie, staring daggers at her for the question. "I am sorry, Bill. I did not mean this question to be rude."

"I know. I know. I am sorry too. This has nearly killed her mother." His shoulders and head sank defeated by the stress of the situation

"If we are going to find your daughter, then we have to ask the tough questions. We may not like some of the answers we find. But they must be asked," she said quietly.

"She was seeing a boy. But as far as we know, they broke up and are now just friends. His name is Steve Elliott. He works on one of the local ranches as a cowhand." He gave her the rest of the information on the ranch and his contact information.

"All right. Let me start gathering some information. I am going to need to get her birth date, social security number, credit cards numbers, etc. I will check to see if anything has been run through on her credit cards. I will talk to some friends at the sheriff's office and start seeing what I can find out. I think I am going to want to talk to everyone that was at that party. Someone has to know something to give us some insight into what happened to Shelby. They might be more willing to talk to me, her father, or the sheriff. I will see what I can find out and be in touch."

Bill got up from the sofa, looking thoroughly defeated from the experience. Ellie felt a twinge in her heart for the man. She knew his loss. Shelby's father seemed to have aged right before her eyes during their discussions. Seeing Bill to the door, she placed a hand on his shoulder and let him know that she would be doing everything in her power to help find his daughter. A slight forced smile came to his lips. He turned and walked away.

Racing back to her computer and phone, Ellie began her search on her first case. This was going to be a tough one, she felt. She had a feeling that before this case was over that it was going to tap every emotion she had. Ellie knew she needed to put those emotions aside and get to work.

Emotions were not going to help her find this man's daughter.

Picking up the phone, she dialed the sheriff's office and asked to speak with Officer Barkley. She was going to have to pull a string or two to get some answers. This is where charm and fortitude were going to come in handy.

"This is Officer Barkley." Sounding just like an officer, she mused to herself.

"Jim. It's Ellie Moore. How are you?" Using all the sweetness in her voice.

"Mrs. Moore? I am good. What can I do for you?" Surprise in his voice.

"Now, Jim. It was Mrs. Moore when you and John Jr. were kids. Now it's Ellie. I need your help on a case I am working on." She went on to explain about Shelby Wallace and having her dad as a new client.

"I had heard a rumor that you had become a private detective. Wasn't sure what to make of it to be honest. I never expected you to jump in this line of work."

"Well, to be honest, after John died, I started looking for something to do, and this type of work always interested me. Do you think you can help me out?" Praying that he would take her seriously.

"It's not my case but let me do some checking. It might be late this afternoon. I have to be up in court here in a bit. Give me your fax number, and I will try to get the report over to you before dinner." Now sounding a bit rushed.

Ellie gave him her fax number and cell number and said to say hello to his folks.

This was going to be a long afternoon. Ellie was ready to go to work. In the meantime, she would get a hold of Shelby's credit card company and her bank to see what she could find. But first, a coffee run was in order. Plus she was eager to let Sue know that she got her first case. This would give her a chance, too, to absorb everything and start putting all the information she received from Bill in order. She wanted to go about everything logically and not miss any steps or processes.

This case would be much more than she bargained for and would test her to every limit Ellie had in her. She didn't know it now, but trouble lie ahead.

CHAPTER THREE

Talking to the credit card company and bank lead nowhere.

Frustrated, Ellie sat back in her chair and began to drum her pen on the notepad. Deep in thought, it took Ellie a minute to realize the phone was ringing.

"Moore Detective Agency."

"Ellie. It's Jim. You going to be in your office for a bit? I think we need to talk." A nervous edge in his voice.

"Sure. I will be here for a bit. Just going over some stuff." Wondering why his tone suddenly made her nervous.

"Great. Give me twenty minutes, and I will be right over."

Click. And the line was dead.

Ellie sat, staring at the phone for a moment and began to wonder what that was all about. Something was up. She could feel the butterflies in her stomach begin to rise. Looking up at the clock on the wall, it was just after 5:30 p.m. No use getting all excited. She would just have to wait and see what Jim had to tell her. Instinct was telling her that she wasn't going to like what she was going to hear.

*****

Jim arrived shortly after six. He came into the office and sat in the chair. Sliding the folder in his hands across the desk toward Ellie, she reached out as it slid toward her. Jim sat back in the chair and let out a deep sigh. Ellie tried to read his face and see what he was thinking. She decided to wait and let him begin.

"Ellie. I am afraid you have bitten off more than you can chew on this one. Looks like your girl was being investigated for some time now. She was dating a young man from up in Wolf Creek who has some drug ties."

Ellie didn't say anything. She listened and let Jim continue, just giving a nod now and then to let him know she was listening.

"Seems she had been seeing this Elliott character. Steve Elliott. He has been suspected in being involved in a meth ring, operating out of the area. So far, no one has been able to get anything on him. We have not been able to find much on his background either. Seems he just showed up here in and began to work. No one knows much about him and that makes us nervous.

"The drug task force hasn't been able to get anything on him either. They have been trying to get some information on him from some of our local informants and nothing has come of it.

"Seems there is one thing that has a bit nervous. We did have a local informant who was doing some checking on him. Our informant suddenly went quiet and wouldn't give a reason. Then our informant up and disappears. We have not been able to find hide nor hair of the fella. We don't like it. Something has been going on out there in Wolf Creek, and we are trying to get to the bottom of it."

"What does this have to do with Shelby?"

"Seems a person that sounded a lot like Ms. Wallace made a call into our tip line at the drug task force. The person simply said they had some information on Steve Elliott and the owner of the ranch he works for in Wolf Creek. The owner of the ranch goes by the name of Howard Long. Mr. Long is a native of California and has long been suspected of being the head of a major meth cartel out there. No one has been able to get any information on him either. Seems his background is a ghost too.

"We think that Elliott is working for Long as an enforcer. We are getting tips that something major is in the works, and now, we have two people who could possibly help us nail these guys disappear.

"It doesn't look good any way you look at. I want you to know that you might be getting yourself involved here with some major players. If that's the case, then you need to know what you're up against."

"What makes you think it was Shelby that called in the tip?" Her interest now thoroughly piqued.

"At first, we didn't know for sure. However, a trace is put through on all the calls that come into the tip line. Seems the call was traced back to Ms. Wallace's cell phone."

"Well, now. That does make things interesting."

"I am afraid you're not going to find much in that report. Just your basic information and inventory of what was found in the car. The forensics team went through the vehicle and didn't find any evidence of foul play."

"But with her call in to the tip line, then it does start to make it all look pretty interesting." Fingers drumming the desk. Ellie resting her chin in her hand in thought.

"We think that Shelby either found out, or saw something that got her worried. Worried enough to make a call anyway. Either way, with her missing, it doesn't look good." Looking concerned and tired, Jim sunk into the comfortable chair much farther.

He began to speak again. "I am afraid that this is all part of our ongoing investigation and has to remain between the two of us. This is the reason I came to your office. You can't let anyone know what I told you. I don't want to see you get hurt on this one. I worried that you might get into this and ask the wrong question to the wrong person and get yourself in a bit of a mess or worse"

Ellie's head jerked up at the warning. Looking across the desk at Jim, she could see the concern written in his eyes. Looks like her first case was going to be a tough one and a dangerous one at that. *Well, I wanted excitement and looks like I am getting it.* She began to wonder if she was biting off more than she could chew.

As Jim left her office, she found herself, chewing on the end of her pen in thought. Maybe Shelby wasn't missing but hiding. If she found out something about his drug ring, it would make sense to want to hide. Hopefully, something worse hadn't happened to the girl. Ellie found herself shuddering at that idea and tried to remove it from her mind. She would need to interview her friends. Girls talk and maybe one of them knew more than they were saying.

Time to talk to Stacy and Lynn. They were the last ones to see her.

*****

Driving out to Wolf Creek.

Ellie found Stacy's home easy enough. Her parents had a beautiful log home, overlooking Holter Lake. Pulling into the driveway, Stacy was standing in the doorway, waiting for her. The girl didn't look eager to talk, standing there with her hands shoved deep in her pockets. Ellie thought this might be a tough nut to crack. Either that or this girl knew more than what she had previously said in her statements to the sheriff and Shelby's father.

The girl said a quiet hello and lead Ellie into a study just off the entrance. Looking around the room, Ellie saw that this girl grew up with no shortage of money. The study was two stories high flanked with tall book shelves. Glancing at some of the titles on the shelves, she saw some rare additions that had to cost a penny or two over her budget. It was a library collection most would envy. She led her over to some reading chairs that weren't quite your typical reading chairs But more of an overstuffed calfskin-leather-covered high-class BarcaLounger. Looking at the chairs, they probably cost almost as much as her car. The room was definitely built to impress for those brought into its presence.

Ellie sat down in the comfortable chair. She decided to take the tact that she would wait for the girl to speak. This was a tactic she had learned in her schooling. It would give the person being quiet the upper hand. It set a level of dominance between two people. Ellie felt like she would need the upper hand with this girl, but she also wanted to build a level of trust.

"I am not sure I have anything that can help you out with Shelby's disappearance," the girl said rather quickly.

"First, let's get to know one another. Then we can get into all that. Are there any questions that you would like to ask of me?" She had heard the girl say Shelby's disappearance and began to wonder why she used that term. It was an odd and interesting way to start a conversation. Most people thought Shelby's was probably murdered, but this girl specifically said disappearance.

"Not really. You just don't look or act the way you see private detectives on TV."

"Well, that's probably true. I think I am going to take that as a compliment!" she said with her best grandmotherly smile. She could see the girl begin to relax in the chair. It was amazing what a simple smile could do.

"How did you end up doing this?" Stacey asked, relaxing further back into her chair.

"Boredom, my dear. My life was at a crossroads, and I needed some excitement added to my life," she answered simply and honestly, hoping to further the trust.

"Cool," the girl said with little enthusiasm.

"How long have you known Shelby?" Simple questions first.

"We have been best friends since second grade."

"That's a long time." She could see Stacy smile at the thought of their friendship and the compliment.

Ellie decided to start her questions. "Can you tell me about that night and what you girls decided to do and did?"

"Not much. We drove around for bit, then ended up down at the ball field at the school."

"Where did you all drive around?"

"Let's see. We mostly drove around up at the lake and the campgrounds. We were wanting to see if any cute guys were camping up at the lake." A blush filled her cheeks on her last statement.

"Did you find any? Cute guys, that is."

"No. Just a couple of high school kids with their parents. We stopped and swam for a bit down at Log Gulch Campground. They have a nice sandy beach there, and more people tend to come down and swim there. It's not so rocky on the beach like at the other campground."

"Did Shelby talk to anyone, or seem to argue with anyone while you were there?" Ellie was trying to move the conversation along.

"No. We were all together. Steve drove by with his friends, and they stopped by for a minute. But there wasn't an argument with anyone."

"Okay. So there were no arguments. Are you talking about Steve Elliott? Didn't he and Shelby just recently break up, or quit seeing each other? How was their conversation at the beach?" There his name again. The man keeps popping up everywhere.

"They didn't argue, but Shelby tried to end the conversation quickly." A nervous edge back in her voice.

"Why did she try to end the conversation so quickly?" *Now I am getting to the meat of the matter.*

"Shelby didn't want to see Steve anymore. He kept coming around, and she had been trying to avoid him."

"Why was she trying to avoid him?" *Odd. Maybe it was just a young lover's thing?*

"Shelby said that sometimes Steve was too intense. When he got that way, it made her nervous. Shelby wanted to have fun, and Steve would get in one of his moods and ruin her fun times." Stacy sounded like she was avoiding the answer.

"What specifically made her nervous?"

"Well. Shelby said he would get jealous of other guys when she talked to them. He started wanting to know where she was at and what she was doing all the time. Sometimes she felt like he was keeping too much of an eye on her."

"Do you think he was stalking her?" Right to the heart of the matter.

"I wouldn't say that, but he did show up at strange times. But then it's a small town, so you're bound to run into one another sooner or later."

"Was this while they were dating, or after they broke it off?" Ellie was beginning to get the sinking feeling that somehow this Elliott character was involved in this whole thing. Her gut feeling was telling her to look more closely at their relationship.

"Both," Stacy said too quickly.

"Sounds like Shelby was becoming afraid of Steve? Do you think Shelby would take off on her own to get away from Steve?"

The girl's mouth suddenly fell open as though maybe she had said too much. Stacey didn't say anything, so Ellie continued.

"I think you know more than what you're telling me. You need to trust me that I am here to help Shelby and not get her into trouble. If Shelby is in trouble in some way, then you need to let me know. I can help her and have friends who can help her and keep her safe. If Steve is the reason that she is hiding, then I need to know." Ellie laid it all out on the table.

The girl bounded from her chair, saying, "I am sorry that I can't help you anymore." It was obvious the conversation was over. Ellie handed the girl her card and walked out the front door and back to the car. She was about to turn around to say goodbye when the door closed quickly behind her.

Once in her car, Ellie backed out of the driveway. It had been an interesting conversation. She knew now that the girl was not missing but in hiding. That had become obvious. Ellie drove and wondered if she jumped too quickly at the end of their conversation. It was obvious the girl wasn't ready to say more, yet she hoped that by giving her the business card that she would use it. Something definitely had to have happened for the girl to feel she needed to hide.

When Ellie arrived at Shelby's friend Lynn's house. It was abundantly clear that the girl no longer had anything to say to her. In the time it took to drive from Stacy's parents place on Holter Lake and reach Lynn's house over on Highway 434, the phone lines must have been burning. Lynn wouldn't even come to the door. Her mother answered the door, saying that her daughter was terribly upset and now was not a good time to talk. Ellie barely had time to give the mother her business card before the door was closed in her face.

Ellie said loudly through the door, "I am here to help the girls. I know that something bad is going on. I can't help if the girls don't talk to me. My number is on the card. Please get your daughter to use it. I really want to help them out and bring Shelby home!" She could hear the footsteps move away from the door, hoping that her plea had not fallen on deaf ears and that the mother would talk some sense into the girl.

*****

Getting back to her office, Ellie stretched out on her comfy sofa and tried to piece the afternoon's events out in her mind. First, she found it odd that Stacy had specifically used the word disappearance.

There were so many other words that the girl could have used to explain what she thought had happened. But she had started off the conversation with that word. Second, when she mentioned quite by chance if there was a reason for Shelby to hide from Steve, the girl suddenly looked like she had let the cat out of the bag. That one, thankfully, didn't have a good poker face. Third, the other girl, Lynn, would no longer even talk to her. It was strange in itself. After all, she was hired by Shelby's father, and you think her best friends would be jumping at the chance to help?

Something was definitely going on with these girls, and since she couldn't sleep anyway, it was time to take a ride back up to Wolf Creek and do a little tailing of the girls. Ellie walked to the back room and grabbed her go bag with all her equipment in it. She set the bag on the desk and started to prepare for her first stake out. She checked through the bag to make sure everything was there.

Binoculars. Check.

Camera and lenses. Check.

Handheld video camera. Check.

Digital tape recorder. Check.

Flashlights. Check.

Extra batteries for everything. Check.

Ellie grabbed the bag and headed to her car. She would stop at the house and change vehicles and drive John Sr.'s old Ford Explorer with the tinted windows. The girls wouldn't know this car, and she doubted they would expect her in this kind of vehicle. She grinned. Besides, what would a sweet old lady be doing driving a big truck like this?

After picking up the other vehicle, she made a quick stop at the store to pick up a few things to nibble on before she headed out. Might be a long night, and it was better to be prepared than wishing she had made a stop earlier.

CHAPTER FOUR

In a cabin deep in the woods outside Wolf Creek.

Shelby paced around the cabin, wondering if this had been such a good idea. How long was she going to have to stay in this mice-infested cabin? She began to wonder how she had gotten herself into such a mess. She knew her parents must be worried to death over her, but she didn't see any other way. She wanted them to be safe at least.

At least tonight, Stacy and Lynn were supposed to come and see her, so she would not have to be alone all the time. She hoped they would bring some more food. Looking over at the bare shelves, Shelby began to wonder if she was going to have to try and catch some fish out of the creek.

They had to come up with a better plan because she couldn't stay out here forever. The first night she got here, she remembered she had barely slept at all. Outside the cabin, she could hear the coyotes howling, and it scared her to death. It was as if they knew she was in the cabin and were just teasing her to come outside and play. Their calls gave her another uneasy feeling topped by the nervousness and fear she had already felt.

Now she enjoyed listening to the coyotes' call. She remembered her dad, telling her that the coyotes would yip and call to one another to let each know where they were at. They wouldn't call if someone was on their turf or home territory. Shelby now looked at the pack of coyotes as her personal alarm system. Now the coyotes made her feel safe.

Plus Stacy had called her on the throwaway cell phone they got her. She wondered who this lady was that had come around asking questions. Stacy had told her that the lady was hired by her father, but how could she know? It may have been another one of Steve's tricks to get her to come out of hiding. She thought she would have to find out more when the girls got to the cabin. Shelby asked to the girls to bring the wireless laptop with them so she could look up the lady. Thank God, this cabin was located close to the cell tower off Highway 200. Otherwise she would be completely cut off from the world.

It was amazing as it was that their plan worked at all. Shelby would drop off the girls and leave her car abandoned at the end of Little Wolf Creek Road. Shelby then walked the nine to ten miles to the cabin in the dark. Fear that evening had kept her moving. Praying the whole way that no one would see her and that she wouldn't run into a bear, eating choke cherries alongside the darn road. It had taken her almost the entire evening to get to the cabin. She laughed about it now that she had almost walked right past the cabin in the dark. There was no moon out, and she had barely kept to the road as it was. It was fine until she had gotten past the eight-mile marker. Then the road isn't maintained by anyone. Walking on the washed out and the rough road made her keep feeling like she had wandered off into the woods.

It had been one of those moonless dark Montana nights too. Her eyes barely adjusted to see somewhat in the dark. She really felt pity for those who spent their entire lives in the dark and blind. She admired them now as she sat back on the porch. Their strength to go through their whole lives and not be able to see. If they could do that, then she knew that evening that she could find a cabin in the woods.

Shelby sat back in the rocking chair on the porch and began to think about Steve. They had so much fun when they first started dating. It had been nice to date a guy that had a little money and could take her out to eat one in a while. Sure, they mostly went down to the Frenchmen in Wolf Creek, or to Craig to get a burger, but it was still nice to be taken out somewhere. All the other guys she dated were broke high school kids with no money, and all they ever did was sit around that stupid baseball field down at the school. It got pretty boring of doing the same thing all the time. But she just chalked it up to life and living in a small town such as Wolf Creek. It's not like

Wolf Creek was some bustling metropolis. It was just a small fishing town banked on the Missouri River and Holter Lake.

Steve had been great for the first couple of months of their relationship. He seemed like a lot of fun to be around and was the first serious relationship that Shelby had had out of high school. Then things started to get funny. Steve would start asking where Shelby was and who she was with. He started following her and checking up on her all the time. It got creepy. Things had gone well until then. Shelby didn't want to be checked up on for doing nothing. *"Geez. How much trouble could she get into in this little town?"*

Then there was that night at the ranch.

Steve had gotten a call from Howard, saying that he needed him back out at the ranch. Shelby and Steve had been down at the Frenchman, having a burger and fries when he called. Steve had gotten somewhat agitated by the phone call and told Shelby that they needed to stop out at the ranch before going out to the lake. Shelby had really thought much of it because it seemed that Howard was always calling and bitching at Steve for something. They had hurried and finished their burgers quickly and headed back out to the ranch.

When they had gotten out to the ranch. Howard was waiting and standing out on the front porch of the main house. He had looked quite pissed off and kept looking down at his watch. Steve had pulled up and parked the truck in the front of the house. Steve and Shelby had both gotten out of the truck and walked toward the porch.

"What the hell is she doing here? I told you to finish up and get the hell back here!" Howard yelled from the porch.

"Come on, man. We were on a date. What was I supposed to do? Leave her at the bar?"

"I don't care where you left her! When I say we have business to take care of, then you're to get your ass back here! Alone!" This time, Howard had venom in his voice, and it was no vague threat.

"Sorry. I didn't know." Steve was now talking more to his boots then the man, standing on the porch.

"Put her in the house and keep her there. We got some business down in the barn. *Get moving!*"

Shelby had hurriedly followed Steve into the house. Howard had never pretended to like her, but tonight he was acting even more rude. Steve made Shelby promise to stay in the house and that he would be back soon. He had led her into the den and told her to watch some TV and that he shouldn't be long. Shelby just numbly agreed and took the remote and sate in the chair. Something was going on, and it obviously made Steve a bit nervous too. Leave it to Howard to ruin another one of their dates. She didn't know why Steve didn't just look for another job. What did she care? She was going to break up with him anyway. Howard could have Steve all to himself then.

Steve left the den and headed out side. She turned on the television after hearing the porch door close. Sitting in the chair, she began to think. Steve had never acted that way with her before. He genuinely looked scared when he made her promise to stay in the house. That was something new. He never asked her that before? Shelby turned on the TV and started watching the news channel that was already on. She was bored and got up to look around the room. She had wondered over by the French doors that led out to a side porch when she heard rough voices, yelling and hollering. She quickly muted the TV and cracked the door to the side porch.

From her vantage point, she could see the barn and the front doors were open. She couldn't see who was all in the barn. But she could see the shadows dance across the front entrance. It looked and sounded to be three people having a really heated discussion. She could hear Steve and Howard's voices but didn't recognize the third person. Slowly, she crept across the side porch and down the stairs. She was going to see what was happening out in that barn. "Didn't it seem like every time a person needs to be quiet? They hit every board that squeaks." Shelby kind of laughed to herself.

Slowly moving across the lawn toward the barn, she made sure to stay in the shadows and moved along a horse trailer that was parked along the driveway to the barn. She could hear both Howard and Steve, talking to the guy. It was obvious they were angry, and she had never heard Steve talk to someone like that. The hate and anger in his voice frightened Shelby. Quickly and quietly, she moved from the shadow of the horse trailer to the side of the barn. Seeing an open stall door, she crept inside. From here, she could see through the thick rough-hewn timbers of the horse stall. She had a perfect view of the three men in the walkway between the stalls.

The man, whose voice she didn't recognize, sat tied to a chair. His face was swollen and bruised and looked like he had been beaten badly. When he spoke, it was with a slur due to the swelling in his mouth and face. She could hear their words clearly now from her hiding spot.

Howard spoke, "What the hell did you think you were doing, calling the tip line? You didn't think we would find out about it?"

He hit the man's face with the back of his hand as he finished the question. Blood flew from the man's mouth and landed on a board not far from her. It was obvious that Howard didn't really want an answer. He was enjoying beating the man. The smile on his face was eerily vacant.

Shelby was surprised to see Steve not move to help the man. Steve had the man's hair gripped in his hand and had the man's head pulled back. Finally letting go, he threw the man's head forward. Blooding now running from the man's mouth and spilling into his lap. The man continued to try and give an explanation, but his words just came out in a jumble of spit and blood.

Shelby turned around and slid against the boards of the stall to her butt. She was stunned and shocked by what she was seeing.

Hearing the click of gun metal. She turned around to see Howard, holding a pistol in his hand. The weapon was pointed directly at the man's head. Shock didn't allow her to really hear what Howard or Steve were saying. Instead, she looked at the man strapped to the chair. The man's eyes briefly met hers. It was the look of a man that knew he was going to die. She wanted to reach out and help the man, but she knew that they would kill her too.

Again, she met the captive man's eyes. She held his look as the gun fired in Howard's hand. Shelby threw a hand over her mouth to stifle the scream that was boiling inside her. The man head lay slumped over the back of the chair. Part of his head lay on his shoulder. She knew he was dead.

Her mind began to race. They couldn't find her here. She was supposed to be in the house, watching television. She ran from the stall, stopping briefly along the horse trailer. She looked back at the barn before running to the side porch. She had just seen a man shot in the head before her very eyes. The man knew she had been watching from the horse stall. God, would she ever be able to get the look in his eyes out of her head?

Stumbling up the stairs of the side porch, she threw herself at the French doors, trying to get them open. It took her a moment to realize she was trying to open the wrong side of the doors. She grasped the other door handle and turned. Nothing. This time, she turned it harder. The door handle moved, and she could hear the latch open. She flung the door open.

Quickly trying to grab a hold of it before it slammed into the wall, letting everyone know she had been outside. Barely reaching it before it hit the wall, she shut the door quickly and quietly. Throwing herself into the chair and returning the volume to the TV just as she heard the front door open and close.

Steve came into the den to see how she was doing. Acting as though nothing at all bad had just happened in the barn. He noticed that she was shaking and asked her if she was all right? Shelby tried to remain calm and said that she was just cold. Steve grabbed a blanket off the ottoman and covered her legs and kissed her on the cheek.

As he was kissing her, Shelby could see flecks of blood across Steve's shirt. Trying to hold back the feeling to vomit right there. She said thank you and covered up more with the blanket. She then asked if he was almost finished and that she was getting tired. She said she thought she might be coming down with something. Maybe it was that burger that hadn't settled right with her? Steve told her that it would just be a little bit longer, and he and Howard were just finishing up some business.

Business?

That's all that was to him?

He just watched his boss kill a man, and all it was is business? Her mind was racing, wanting to scream at him. How could he be so callous? He just watched a man die, but then he had done nothing to stop or prevent it. So this was his job for Howard? He was nothing more than a lackey who did what Howard wanted. He didn't seem sad or scared to have just seen the murder of a man?

Shelby began to wonder how many other times Steve had been in the same position. Looking up at the man before her, she knew she didn't know this person at all. She didn't want to know this person at all. He was a killer plain and simple and so was his boss. She fought the urge to hit him and slap him and ask why. She wanted to cry. To run. To just get the hell out of there as quickly as possible.

Sitting in the chair, she hadn't notice Steve even left the room. She barely remembered him, saying that he should be down in about twenty minutes. Noticing he was gone, Shelby began to cry. It all just came rushing out of her. She wept for a man she did not know. She wept for herself and the situation she was now in. How the heck was she going to get out of this?

*****

Later on, after what seemed like hours, Steve had come back into the den. Shelby had fallen asleep covered up in the chair. The stress and adrenaline had crashed down on her, putting her right to sleep. When Steve lightly shook her shoulder to wake her. Shelby jumped from the chair ready to fight like a wild cat. Steve stood there, looking at her, laughing. Shelby then mentioned he scared the heck out of her. She set the blank back down on the chair and followed Steve out to the truck. She was no longer in a talking mood or a date mood. She simply told him she wanted to go and that she wasn't feeling well.

When they reached her parent's house to drop her off, Steve had turned on the interior light for her to get her things and give her a kiss good night. Shelby found herself, staring at the specs of blood that dotted his shirt. Steve looked down and simply said he must have gotten some ketchup on shirt at the bar. She looked up and gave him a half smile and simply got out of the truck.

Steve rolled down the window and said, "What? No kiss?"

Shelby half mumbled an apology and turned and walked to the house. She hoped he would just write it off as her not feeling well. At this point, she didn't care. She just wanted to get inside and away from this man.

That night, Shelby did not sleep well. She tossed and turned and wept some more. The shower she had taken after she had gotten home had done little to wash away the feelings that had swept over her.

Still sitting out on the porch of the cabin, Shelby looked back at the events that seemed like a million years ago. Yet everything had happened in the last four weeks. Seeing headlights off in the distance, Shelby immediately ran into the cabin to turn off all the lights. She quickly bolted the doors. It was probably only the girls but better to be safe than sorry.

Silently from behind the curtain, she kept watch over the lights that were headed her way. She watched as the vehicle crossed the bridge at the creek and gave a sigh of relief. It was just Stacy and Lynn.

What the three of them didn't notice was Ellie had been following the girls with her lights off. She stopped up on the ridge out of sight. Grabbing her binoculars, she slid quietly from the truck and walked down the ridge line where she would have a good view of the cabin.

Ellie watched as the car with the two girls pulled up to the cabin. She could see the brake lights clearly without the binoculars. A light had turned on in the cabin. She watched in the binoculars as the girl she had been searching for had stepped out onto the deck. A deep sense of relief swept over Ellie.

However, another thought crept into her mind, *Why was this girl hiding in the first place?*

Walking back up to the old Ford Explorer, Ellie climbed into the driver's seat and sat for a moment to catch her breath. She realized that she needed to get back into the karate classes that she took before John had passed away. A little exercise would do her some good for sure. Plus in this line of work, her karate skills needed to bring back up to speed. John Jr. had made her take the classes after her purse had been stolen at the Women's Park in downtown Helena. He wanted her to be safe and know how to defend herself. Ellie baulked at the idea originally but then came to realize that she liked the classes and the instructor.

Starting the engine, she decided to drive down the ridge line for a closer look. She put the truck in its lowest gear and began to roll slowly down the mountain road. The low gear of the engine allowed Ellie to not have to use her brakes and give away her position. Getting down to the end of the road, Ellie decided to park her vehicle some hundred yards or so from the cabin. She didn't want to scare Shelby off but thought a surprise visit was in order. Grabbing the flashlight from her backpack, she quickly turned it on and off to make sure it was working. From under the seat, she tucked the 9 mm pistol in her purse. She probably wouldn't need the gun, but she was deep in the mountains. *And you never know what lurked behind the bushes*, she thought.

Making her way through the brush back to the small woods road, she began to wish she hadn't park the truck behind those firs. She would be picking pickers and stickers from her legs for the next week. Keeping the flashlight in her hand but turned off, she made her way up the road. Walking slowly, she was alert for any stray bears that may be feasting on berries in the bushes. For a moment, she thought, *what am I doing out here?* Then she did a quick mental chastising of herself. She wanted adventure, and now, she was getting it.

About twenty-five feet from the cabin, she stopped and hid behind a pile of stacked firewood. From inside the cabin, she could hear the talking of the girls. Quietly, she moved from the pile of wood to the front door. Hoping the wood stairs would not give her away, she tested the first board with her foot. It didn't budge or squeak, so she tried the next. This board didn't squeak either. Just as she put her foot onto the deck, the board she chose gave her away. It let out the creak of an old rusty door that needed oiling.

Suddenly, the cabin door flew open, and Ellie found herself, looking down the barrel of a shot gun. Poor Ellie thought she was going to faint dead away at the sight of the gun. She had to grab the handrail on the stairs to steady herself. With one foot on the stairs and the other on the deck, she already felt off-balance.

"Who the hell are you, and what do you want?" She heard a fear in the voice of Shelby as the girl still kept the gun pointed right at her.

"The girls know who I am. I was hired by your father to try and find out what happened to you. I am here to help. Honestly. Would you please put the gun down so that we can talk?" Ellie felt like she was grasping at straws.

To the left in the cabin window, Ellie could see Stacy and Lynn, peeking their heads out from behind the curtain.

From inside the cabin, she heard one of the girls say, "It's all right. She is that woman that came and talked to me at the house."

Ellie assumed it was Stacy since she had been unable to talk to Lynn.

Shelby lowered the gun and simply said, "Come on. Get inside."

"Thank you," Ellie said breathlessly. She didn't let go of the handrail until she was sure that her knees weren't going to buckle.

"Sorry about the gun thing, but I didn't know who you are. You shouldn't go sneaking up on people who don't want to be found," Shelby chastised.

Ellie entered the cabin and saw the two girls, standing near the window. If their eyes had been filled with daggers, then Ellie would be dead as a door nail. She smiled at the girls and moved toward the table.

Looking at Shelby, she said, "Do you mind if I have a seat before I fall over. I have never had a gun pulled on me before. I think I need a minute to gather my wits about me."

As Ellie sat down and looked around the little cabin, the three girls moved to the table, and all took up seats around the table. Everyone was seated now. Ellie thought she should and would break the silence.

"Your father hired me to find you. He is very worried, and your mother is at the end of her rope with worry."

Shelby replied, "I know. I can only imagine. I feel so bad about all this, but I really had no other choice. I didn't know what to do."

"How about you tell me what is really going on so that we can formulate a plan and get you out of whatever mess you're in?" Ellie asked.

"I don't think you or anybody else can help me," Shelby said and looked dejected.

"Shelby. Shelby, look at me. I am here to help you. You would be surprised by looking at me, but I have a few tricks up these old sleeves of mine!" Ellie reached out and put her hand on the girl's shoulder. This girl looked traumatized, and Ellie knew she needed to do what she could to comfort her and lighten the mood.

Lynn, who had remained silent through the exchange, spoke up, "You might as well, Shell. At this point, what else have you got to lose? We are not coming up with any great ideas. Besides, you can't stay hiding in this cabin forever. Sooner or later, my folks are going to take a ride out and find you here."

Shelby looked around the table. First, looking at each of the girls who were her best friends. Each friend nodded in agreement. Then she looked at Ellie and held her eyes right at her, looking at Ellie to see if Shelby could really trust her, or should trust her.

"At this point, all that is left is for them to kill me," Shelby said, defeated.

Ellie looked up with surprise and said, "I think it's time you tell me all that has happened to you. You need to start from the beginning and tell me everything. Then we can decide what to do."

Over the next hour, Shelby paced around the small one room cabin, telling Ellie everything that had happened to her. She started with dating Steve, to what had happened in the barn, all the way up to her abandoning her car, and walking all the way out to the cabin in the dark. Ellie only asked the occasional pertinent question but tried to remain silent and let the girl tell her story. It was difficult for the girl to get it all out, and Ellie let her take her time. She knew this was the first time that she really had to recount what had happened over the past couple of months and that it couldn't be easy.

One thing for sure was that she knew now that she had to protect all the girls. Shelby's friends also knew what had happened in the barn and that made them loose ends. If someone were to find out that Stacy and Lynn knew about the informant being killed, their lives would be in danger. Ellie brought this to their attention, but the girls had made a good point.

"Don't you think if we all just up and disappear that Steve and Howard will figure out that something is going on? Shelby was at the ranch house that evening, and it won't take them long to figure it all out," said Stacy.

"You have a point there," Ellie spoke.

"It would be better for us to be home and keep up the appearances of two best friends worried and sad about their missing best friend," Lynn said with conviction.

"Yes. But you two have to remember that you can't tell a soul. If you were to accidentally mention this to anyone, and it got back to Steve and Howard, then you both would be dead for sure," Ellie pulled no punches as she spoke. She figured the girls needed to know what they were up against in all of this.

"I don't want them to be any more involved than they already are in this." Shelby looked up and reached across the table and grabbed her best friend's hands, gathering strength from one another in a very tough situation.

While they gathered strength, Ellie formulated a plan.

"Stacy and Lynn, I want you both to go on how you have been. Don't tell anyone about our meeting tonight, or that you know that Shelby is still alive. I am going to take Shelby with me, but I think it's going to be better for everyone that you both don't know where she is going. This way, if something happens, and someone asks you about her, you can honestly say that you don't know. Don't worry now, girls. I am going to do everything in my power to keep your friend safe."

Ellie reached out and took Shelby's hand in hers and gave her best motherly smile she could muster. Talking to Stacy and Lynn, she got them up and their coats on and got them walked to their car. She hugged them both and promised that she would be in touch with them as soon as possible. Tears fell from their eyes. Neither girl said a word. They did as instructed and got into their car and headed back up the mountain to Wolf Creek and home.

Ellie watched as the taillights of the vehicle headed back up the ridgeline. Waiting until they were completely out of sight, she then turned and headed back up to the cabin where Shelby was standing in the door. She climbed the stairs and walked across the deck with her arms open. Shelby almost fell into her arms.

This time, it was Ellie, giving the comfort. It felt good to be giving someone love and understanding. In the last three years, she had received more than her fair share. It was time to give a little of that love back. Ellie began to feel a real purpose renewed in her life. This was why she had chosen this new path. She continued to hold the girl and give her the attention she needed.

CHAPTER FIVE

Ellie got Shelby packed up and got them both headed back to the Ford Explorer. She was glad that she had chosen this truck this evening. She would be able to hide Shelby in the back seats, and the car windows were tinted. If anyone was looking, they would have a very difficult time trying to see through the windows in the dark.

Walking through the dark again was no easy task. Their eyes had become accustomed to the light of the cabin, and it made the darker night even blacker. Ellie had almost stepped off the bridge. Shelby had clung so tight to her shirt that it made it hard to walk. Ellie finally had to stop and take her hand in hers so she could walk properly.

Finally, they reached the area where Ellie had left the vehicle. She hadn't seen anyone or lights, so she figured it was safe to turn on the flashlight. Plus she knew she wasn't going to find the truck again with some sort of light.

This is where some good night-vision goggles would come in handy, Ellie thought.

She would look into those soon just in case she were to be in another situation like this aging. She laughed to herself at the thought of her a fifty-five-year-old grandmother, running through the Montana wilderness dressed like a commando. Ellie thought they would be a nifty little tool to have in her go bag.

They reached the truck with only a few minor scrapes and trips over brush. Ellie had accidentally stepped in a cow manure and shined the flashlight down to her feet. In any other situation, this would have made her wrinkle her nose with disgust. Tonight, with all the stress of the situation, she found herself with a case of the church giggles. The ones where you know it is neither the time nor the place to laugh, but you just can't help yourself. Both Ellie and Shelby lay against the side of the truck, having a well-needed laugh. It brought a little relief to an evening filled with stress.

Off in the distance, they both heard a vehicle, moving down the mountain road toward their position. Ellie grabbed open the back door and practically threw Shelby to the floor. This wasn't a time for gentleness. Ellie grabbed the blanket off the back seat and covered Shelby with it. She now hoped that the truck was deep enough in the bushes to not be seen. Shelby didn't seem to mind the rough treatment. She was moving just as quickly to get hidden and get out of sight.

Ellie climbed in the driver's seat and got the keys in the ignition. This was no little feat with hands that were now shaking. She looked in the back seat and said she was going to let the vehicle pass by and get out of sight before moving. Ellie didn't want to give away her position. Ellie was getting that feeling in her stomach again. Something was telling her not to move. Why was someone on this road so late at night? Not exactly the road you want to be driving down in the dark of night. Ellie told Shelby not to move.

The truck coming down the hill was a large club cab of a vehicle. Ellie couldn't quite make out what kind of vehicle it was from that distance yet. The eerie thing about the truck was that it was moving so slow down the mountain. Even the girls in their car that was much lower to the ground had moved quicker up the hill. This truck and its passengers were looking for something or someone. Ellie started recited prayers in her head. She prayed they wouldn't be able to see their vehicle. She hoped that none of the windows would give a reflection to the oncoming lights of the truck.

Slipping silently down the hill, the truck made it to the creek crossing and slowly drove right past the Explorer. They hadn't been seen, but they weren't out of the woods yet. Just after passing the hidden truck. A spotlight came on from the searching vehicle. It was scanning the area, and she hoped they would not scope behind their vehicle.

Ellie had Shelby sit up to see if she recognized the truck. Ellie could see immediately that Shelby had recognized the vehicle just outside her window. Ellie had to throw her hand over Shelby's mouth to quiet the girl from screaming. Right now, a scream would not be advantageous to their situation.

Throwing herself back to the floor of the Explorer, Shelby started saying, "Oh my god! Oh my god! Oh my god!"

Ellie grabbed Shelby's shoulder and said, "What is it?"

"It's Steve's truck! He must be looking for me, or someone told him that I am out here!" the words came out from Shelby with fear and cracking in her voice.

"Who else knew you were out here?" Ellie asked but no response.

Ellie watched as the truck slowly pulled up in front of the cabin. Gunfire erupted and lit up the night. Whoever was in that vehicle was shooting up the very cabin they were just in. Both women let out a scream at the sounds of weapons being fired. It shook both of them. They had just missed dying by only a few minutes.

The gunfire continued until it sounded as if they were out of ammunition. Shelby had Ellie's hand in hers. She was gripping it so tightly that Ellie finally had to pull away from the pain. Rolling the down the window, Ellie's ears searched for any sound, coming from the direction of the cabin. She heard what sounded like a door being kicked in and more gunfire inside the cabin.

With her window down, she could hear two different people distinctly. Shelby must have heard them, too, because she said that it was Howard and Steve. She could hear the swearing in the quiet of the darkness that now surrounded them.

"Fuck! We must have missed her. You need to find that bitch and get rid of her before she is able to talk to anyone else. Get rid of that old woman she is with too! I don't want to see or hear anything coming from either of them!" they could hear Howard say.

"Don't worry about it. That bitch isn't going to live long enough to double-cross me! Next time she looks through a stall, I bet that bitch will think twice!" Shelby could hear Steve talk with a vengeance in his voice.

Car doors slammed, and they heard muffled voices from inside the pickup. Not being able to make out what they were saying, it was obvious to both that they didn't want to find out. The approaching vehicle and its occupants were no longer using their spotlight. Both women hunkered down in the vehicle and again prayed their truck wouldn't be seen on their way out and back up the mountain.

As the truck was about to cross the creek, it stopped. The passenger door opened and out stepped Howard. He took a few steps away from the truck and stood there. Ellie didn't know how much more she could take. The killers were only twenty feet from them. The only thing separating the two parties were a huge grove of chokecherry bushes and few dwindling pine trees. If there had been a moon, they would be caught for sure.

The man outside was still just standing there, and Ellie began to wonder what he was doing. Soon, it became apparent, and she had to again stifle her nervousness that was about to erupt in the form of laughter. The man was peeing. Ellie fought the urge to fire the pistol now in her hand at the man. It would do them no good to give away their position, but it sure would make her feel better. Shelby could tell what Ellie was thinking and placed her hand on her wrist to dissuade Ellie from making a bad move.

In the back of her mind, Shelby knew she, too, wouldn't mind seeing Howard shot right in the balls. Giving him a little taste of his own medicine. The man was a murderer and didn't deserve any pity from her or Ellie.

The sound of a zipper being zipped up, and the shuffle of feet moved back toward the other truck. Both women heard the truck door close, and the truck begin to move forward. They both let out a simultaneous breath of relief. That had been too close of a call. Thank God that Ellie had decided to hide the vehicle and move in to the cabin on foot. Sitting in silence until the truck lights were well out of view, Shelby climbed over the front seat and took her place in the passenger seat. Neither said a word. Both just sat, staring out the front window. They both knew how close they had come to death just now. No words were needed for the time being.

"Well. We obviously can't go the way I came in. They might be checking out all the roads that shoot off from Little Wolf Creek Road. I think it would be too dangerous to go that way," Ellie said aloud to no one in particular.

Shelby spoke up, "If we follow the road past the cabin. It comes out on Highway 200 on the top of Rogers Pass. It's pretty rough. I hope this thing has four-wheel drive."

"It does. You point me in the right direction, and we will get moving." Ellie didn't waste any time starting the vehicle and backing it up onto the woods road that would lead them to safety. She hoped.

Shelby pointed out a couple curves. Ellie couldn't believe the road they were traveling down. It was well rutted and full of small boulders. The way was more of a trail than an actual road. At one point in the road, they had to cross an old washout that was made from the spring melt off. The gully that stood before them was about eight feet deep but looked to have had the sides knocked down from four-wheeler travel. Ellie stopped above the wash for a moment to take in the view before them. She had never driven over roads like these and didn't know if the old Explorer was up to the challenge.

Slowly, she crept the truck into the gully, and just as the front of the truck was headed back up the other side, Ellie stepped on the gas for all it was worth. The truck bounced and jarred them around the cab. Somehow in all the harsh movements, her foot had never left the gas pedal. She continued to keep her foot on the gas as they rounded a sharp curb on the other side of the wash. Getting back to even ground, Ellie stopped and got out of the truck. She needed the fresh air. She really needed a big glass of wine after the night's adventures.

*****

To fill the time and the quiet. Shelby began to tell Ellie that this very road was once used in the old days for wagon and slay travel. It was used as a shortcut when the folks from Wolf Creek would head over to Lincoln, Montana for a dance. Ellie couldn't imagine, traveling down these roads or mountains in a sleigh. The journey must have been quite scary. Shelby had followed Ellie from the vehicle but stopped telling her story. Neither was interested anymore.

After a few moments, Ellie and Shelby looked at one another, standing there in the headlights in front of the truck. Both started to laugh. The road had been one that they hoped they would not have to travel again. It was a laughter filled with relief and stress. They had both just come out of something new to both of them. Neither had been hunted before, and the night's events had caught up to both of them. The laughter was healing and a stress relief after the night's events.

The laughter was a well-needed stress reliever. They both got back in the truck, and Ellie put it in drive and slowly moved forward along the old mountain road.

"The road gets much better now. The phone company maintains it to be able to reach their cell tower. Once we get around the corner, it evens out and should be easy to drive on all the way to the blacktop," informed Shelby. Drawing another breath of relief, Ellie said, "That's good. I think I have had enough off-road thrills for one night!"

The road did indeed level out around the bend just like Shelby had predicted. Ellie picked up a little speed over the well-maintained mountain road. Just as they were getting to the black top, a huge deer jumped out in front of them. Ellie slammed on the brakes to avoid hitting the animal. Little did they know that that animal had just saved their lives. Up ahead, they both saw the flashes of gunfire. By slamming on the brakes to avoid the mule deer, they missed being hit by the bullets by mere feet.

Now Ellie's dander was up. She was tired of being chased. Grabbing the pistol again from her purse, she pointed it out the window and began to fire at the muzzle flashes ahead of them. Firing her weapon at them made them cease-fire momentarily. She stepped on the gas and gunned it to the pavement. She continued to fire the gun as they sped by Steve's truck. Ellie saw that one lucky bullet had taken out one of the truck tires. It had been a lucky shot. She had fired until the gun just clicked in her hand and was out of bullets. It had been a fortunate shot.

Sliding out onto Highway 200, Ellie put her foot on the gas and didn't take it off. They came down off Rogers Pass like they were in an Indy race car except they were headed the wrong way. She had wanted to turn toward Lincoln so she could head over Stemple Pass back to Helena. Instead, they were headed back toward Highway 434 and Wolf Creek. It was the long way around but not much she could do about it now but keep going. Ellie had barely been able to keep control of the vehicle as they slid out onto the blacktop. Neither was she paying attention to which way she was headed. They had been too busy, trying to avoid the gunfire from Steve and Howard.

Ellie raced down Highway 200 as fast as the vehicle would take them.

Getting off the pass, the highway began to straighten out, and she let the vehicle fly. Never had she driven so fast before. She couldn't take time to think about it either. She hoped no more deer would make a surprise visit in front of them. At this speed, it wouldn't end pretty.

She knew that they only probably had a good ten-minute head start while they changed the tire on the truck. She silently hoped she had done more damage to Steve's truck so that they wouldn't be able to follow.

Mulling something over in her head, she began to question how they knew Shelby was there at the cabin. Shelby had said that only Stacy and Lynn were in the know about where Shelby was staying. That had to mean that one of the two girls was a snitch. It was either Stacy or Lynn who had just betrayed their best friend.

Shelby must have been thinking the same thing.

"Stacy or Lynn must have told Steve or Howard where I was? Why would they do that? They are supposed to be my best friends in the whole world. Now I have no one to trust. Plus how did they know I was with you?"

Hurt in every word of her statement.

"Not true. You and I are going to have to trust each other now. Looks like they want us both dead. We have to find somewhere to hide and fast. They are going to be looking for us." Ellie again reached over and grasped a hold of Shelby's hand for a moment.

Suddenly, an idea popped into Ellie's mind. The old fishing cabin on the lake. No one would expect them to go anywhere near the lake. What better way to hide than in plain sight and right under their noses. They never used the cabin much, and very few people even knew Ellie still owned it. It would give them a chance to rest. The place had an old garage where they could hide the Explorer out of sight.

Continuing to look in her rearview mirror, no headlights were appearing in the distance behind them. Ellie continued to keep her foot on the gas and drive as fast as the road way and corners would allow.

Ellie let Shelby know of her plan and got her input. Shelby was a bit nervous being so close to Howard and Steve and Stacy and Lynn. But she agreed that they would never think to look for them there. It would be right under their noses, and they would never expect them to stay so close.

Racing up Beartooth Road that leads to Holter Lake, Ellie crested to hill by the dam and slowed the vehicle down. She didn't want anyone in the upcoming public campground to see a speeding car, driving past and remember it. She slowed to the posted speed limit of thirty-five miles an hour.

Nervously watching her mirrors, she was unable to see any lights.

Reaching the cabins driveway by Gopher Town, she slowed and casually pulled into the driveway. She instructed Shelby to get out of the vehicle and open up the old garage door. Silently, she pulled the vehicle into the garage stall and cut the engine. Just as quickly, Shelby pulled the garage door down behind her. They actually made it to the cabin. Ellie was both surprised and exhausted.

She helped Shelby grab their things and led her out of the garage and into the cabin. They set all their things down on the kitchen table. Not turning on any lights, Ellie led Shelby to the living room, and they both collapsed onto the old sofa. It was old and musty. At that moment, it felt like heaven. They were safe for now.

Adrenaline that had coursed through their bodies for so long was now causing them to crash. It had been a long day and night for both of them. Neither had been in the mood to talk. They just wanted to rest. Tomorrow was another day, and they could each share what they were thinking then. Relaxing on the sofa, both soon drifted off to sleep. It was a well-needed rest after the day's adventures.

In the morning, they would formulate a plan.

CHAPTER SIX

Waking with a jolt. The sun had come up already, and the clock on the wall was saying it was already 10:00 a.m. Wearily, they looked at one another and gave a brief tired smile. Ellie stood up and stretched near the coffee table. Her bones giving off a creaky sound or two. After last night, she figured her body deserved the noise it was sounding off.

Shelby slowly wiped the sleep from her eyes. She had slept so soundly. It was hard to believe that she could sleep so well after the night they had. She stretched her legs across the sofa, not wanting to really move or wake from the first comfort she had had in a while. Shelby decided she was going to stay planted on that old sofa as long as she could. Her mind didn't really want to think of what was to come. Soon, she drifted back off to sleep.

Ellie looked over and saw Shelby, sleeping on the sofa. She decided to let her rest. God knows how long it's been since she got a good night's sleep. It was time she made some phone calls, and the quiet was welcomed just now. She had to come up with a plan. At this moment, she had no idea what she was going to do. Ellie hoped John Sr. was looking down at her and keeping an eye out over her. She and Shelby were going to need every ounce of protection they could get.

Looking around the table in the kitchen. Ellie found some granola bars that she had picked up at the store before leaving Helena. It surprised her that she was actually hungry! But then she hadn't really eaten anything since around lunch yesterday. Her stomach gave the occasional grumble, but the crunchy sound and texture of the granola bar was more for comfort. Searching through the cupboards, she saw nothing to eat.

Ellie would have to get a hold of Sue and see if she could bring them out some groceries. Not really wanting to involve her friend, but they were going to need food. It was either call Sue or starve. Quietly, she stepped out on the front porch overlooking the lake and dialed Sue's number. She quickly filled Sue in on all the night's events. Sue was pretty upset and worried about Ellie and asked her at one point, "What the hell are you going to do?" Ellie simply told her the truth and told her she didn't know at this point. She was still mulling over ideas. For now, they were safe at the old fishing cabin. Sue said she would close the store right away and stop by the store to do some quick shopping. She would be up in Wolf Creek in an hour or two.

The next call was to Jim at the sheriff's department. Of course, he was out on patrol and couldn't be reached, so Ellie left an urgent message with hopes of him, returning the call soon.

Another thing had been bothering Ellie. Shelby had mentioned that the guy Howard and Steve killed had made a call to the tip line at the drug task force. She began to wonder if this was the informant that Jim had spoken about. Also, it began to make sense that if Howard and Steve knew it was the informant who called in the tip, then there had to be a snitch at the task force or in the sheriff's department.

Somehow, someone told Howard and Steve who made the call. Howard must have a lot of money to be buying the information he was getting. First, Shelby is sold out by one or both of her best friends. Second, the informant is dead because of someone ratting him out. Apparently, Howard Long was going to be more of a problem than she originally thought. Ellie decided she would not underestimate him again.

Sitting back in the old recliner in the living room, Ellie thought she would rest her eyes for a bit until Sue arrived with provisions.

Ellie awoke to the sound of someone outside. She moved to the window to see what or who was making the noise. Not seeing anything out the window, her heart began to race. She moved to the kitchen as she saw someone, trying the door handle. It rattled twice. Ellie looked around for a weapon. She found her purse on the table and grabbed her gun. It was still empty from the night before, and her bullets were in the garage in the truck. Whoever was coming through the door wouldn't know this. Bluff. She would just have to use some darn good acting skills.

The kitchen door handle rattled again. Ellie could see the knob turn. Then she heard, "Are you going to let me in, or do I have to stand out here all day?"

Thank God! It was just Sue.

"You about scared me to death!" Ellie said as she walked over to open the door.

Sue stepped inside the cabin and saw the gun in Ellie's hand and dropped the bags she was carrying. At that moment, she realized her friend was in a lot more trouble than she thought. It was also a surprise to see Ellie, of all people, holding a gun.

"One must not be too careful," said Ellie as she slipped the gun back into her purse on the table.

"I guess not," was all Sue could say.

"Did anyone follow you, or see you outside?" Ellie asked.

"Who is going to be following me? No one knows I am here. I didn't even tell Chuck I was leaving."

Something didn't seem right in Sue's last statement. Ellie had a hard time not raising a questioning eyebrow at her friend. Sue never went anywhere without leaving a note, or some sort of message. She was either very worried about her and Shelby, or something's up. Ellie was getting that feeling in her stomach again. These are the times that she wished she would get a clearer message and didn't have to rely on gut instinct. However, she had never known her friend to lie to her.

Screw this, she was going to just ask and get it out of the way. Ellie couldn't worry about Sue, getting mad at her right now. Too much had happened to her in the last twenty-four hours. If there was something wrong, then they could get it out on the table and work through it.

"Okay, Sue. What is going on?" This time she let her eyebrow arch to show her skeptical thoughts.

"What do you mean, 'What is going on?'" Sue quickly turned her back and had gone stiff at the question.

"Sue. We have been friends for years, and I know damn well when you're lying, or not telling the whole truth. Now let's have it." Ellie had walked over to her friend and placed a hand on her shoulder.

Sue shrugged off the hand of her friend and quickly moved around the table. "I am sure I have no idea what you're talking about?" trying more to convince herself then actually being able to dissuade her friend from the truth.

"Sue. You're scaring me now. What is going on? I don't think I can handle much more. Right now, I need my friend."

Sue dropped herself in a kitchen table chair like a lead rock. All the air deflating from her body. Her face was stricken with fear and grief. She suddenly just let it all out, "I think they have Chuck!"

"What do mean they have Chuck?"

"I didn't tell you that when I was at the grocery store that I got a call from an unavailable number. I wasn't going to answer because I don't like to answer calls from an unavailable number. Never know if it's a bill collector or some telemarketer."

"Okay. Okay. Get on with it, Sue. You're rambling." Ellie felt herself, coming apart at the seams.

"The man told me that if I ever wanted to see Chuck again that I needed to tell him where you were at. At first, I played dumb and acted like I had no idea what he was talking about. Then I heard a painful scream in the background that sounded just like Chuck. I screamed at him to let me talk to him. He just laughed at me and told me that if I wanted to see him again that I better find out where you're at and what you know. Then whoever was on the phone hung up.

"There I was in the grocery store. Screaming like a mad woman into my cell phone and crying for my husband!"

"Did he say when he was going to call you back?"

Shelby had been standing near the wall in the background and spoke up, "It's got to be Howard and Steve."

Sue looked at Shelby then spoke, "No. But I got the feeling that he would be calling back soon to get an answer to his question." Sue couldn't look up at her friend. She didn't want to be in the position of feeling like she was betraying her husband, or having to betray her best friend in the world. It was an impossible situation. She now wanted to be back in the coffee shop and not be involved in this mess.

"Let me think. Let me think." Ellie started pacing around the small kitchen.

"Why does she have to come up with any answer?" Shelby spoke again.

"Excuse me?" Ellie said, questioning her idea.

"I said why does she have to come up with an answer? All she needs to tell the man is that she called you but didn't get an answer and left a message to return her call immediately."

"Great idea." A smile forming on Ellie's face.

Sue said, "Now I am lost? Could one of you please fill me in?"

"This is going to buy us some needed time. You can't tell them where we are, or Chuck may end up dead. This way, it's going to give us a chance to find him." Ellie's mind was now spinning on all cylinders.

At the thought of Chuck being killed, Sue lost any remaining composure that she had been holding on too. Her eyes rolled to be back of her head, and she slid from the chair, banging her head on the way to the floor.

Ellie and Shelby ran to her side. Ellie was bending over her. Slapping her face lightly and saying her name, Sue's eyes slowly opened and started to clear. A look of bewilderment came across her face as Sue began to realize now that she was on the floor. A huge smile came across Ellie and Shelby's faces as they realized she had just fainted and would be fine. The whole thing had shook them so suddenly that it felt right to laugh, and they both hugged their friend, lying on the floor.

It took both of them to move Sue to the sofa, and Shelby got a glass of cloudy water from the sink. Bringing it over to Sue, Shelby could see Ellie's mind in deep thought. Letting her think, she handed the glass of water to Sue and told her to drink slowly. Shelby did her best to comfort the woman she had just met.

"My next thought is this. How would Howard and Steve know that you're my friend, or that you were coming here?"

Ellie's face drained of all color. Raising both hands to her cheeks, it suddenly dawned on her. Shelby saw the look on Ellie's face and asked her what happened.

"I was trying to think of how Howard and Steve would know I am friends with Sue, or that I even called her. I only called two people. One call was to Sue. The other call was Jim at the sheriff's office. I was unable to reach Jim, but left him an urgent message to return my call."

"So?" Shelby asked now perched on the edge of the couch.

"The man you saw killed was an informant for the drug task force and had been in contact with the sheriff's department. Someone in that sheriff's department is on the take. And they obviously know me pretty well. I can only think of one person who knew of my friendship with Sue and Chuck. I am not sure why this didn't hit me sooner. I guess I must really need a brick to hit me over the head to see something!"

"Well. Who is it?" Sue and Shelby said almost in unison.

"I can't believe it I didn't see it sooner. It has to be Jim Barkley. When I called him to get some information on you, he made a specific trip to my office and hadn't wanted to speak over the phone. He had told me that the informant had disappeared. How could he have known that already? You didn't see the guy killed until a couple days later. He could have only known that if he was in on it. At the time, I didn't even pick up on it. He and his family have been close friends of ours for years. Jim hung out with my son, growing up." Lost in thought, Ellie couldn't believe that Jim had gone bad. She didn't want to believe it.

CHAPTER SEVEN

Ellie got out some the old hunting maps her husband kept at the cabin. She was looking for a way onto the Howard's ranch without being seen. She had no doubt that they would be watching the frontage road that passed in front of the property that lead up to the ranch house.

She had the maps stretched out across the kitchen table. She hadn't even bothered to move the groceries that had still lay on the table. With the brush of her arms. She sent the food and canned goods, sliding to the floor. Sue and Shelby came into the kitchen and stood behind her as she laid the maps out.

Scouring the maps, Ellie tried to get her bearings of where they were located on the map. She would have never figured it out if the lake and shoreline hadn't been shown on the map. Trying to tell if the squiggly red lines were roads or demarcations of landmarks, it was Sue who said they marked as old forest service roads on the map. Ellie turned around and grabbed her friend's face in her hands and planted a big kiss on her cheek. Letting go, she spun around, laying out her game plan. Sue simply stood back with a shocked smile on her face. Ellie was on a roll!

Tracing Beartooth Road on the map with her finger, she followed the road down to Log Gulch Campground. It looked like there was a road that cut over from Log Gulch Campground to the back of Howard's ranch. Now she hoped the old Explorer was up to some more off road driving. She knew that if they had Chuck, then they would have him at the ranch away from peering eyes.

Looking up at the women who still remained watching her, Ellie laid out her plans. After telling Shelby and Sue what she was planning, she offered them both the sanctuary of the cabin and let them know they didn't have to come with her. In her mind, she hoped they would as there was safety in numbers. Both women said without any hesitation that they should all stick together. Ellie couldn't help but let out a sigh of relief and reached out and grabbed their hands in hers.

Loading up the Explorer with some provisions, Ellie made her way around the garage, looking for things they could use. She almost missed what she would need most to get access to the old forest service road: a bolt cutter. Grabbing it off its place on the wall, Ellie placed the tool in the back with the rest of the provisions that they had loaded into the SUV.

They had decided to wait until dark to get onto the road. This way, it would be much harder for anyone to notice their vehicle and if it was them in it. Lounging around the cabin, they all did their best to pass the time. However, time was no longer their friend.

A phone began to ring in the kitchen.

They all looked at one another quickly.

Fear seeping into their faces.

Almost tripping over one another, they ran to the kitchen to check whose phone was ringing. It was Sue's. Immediately, all color drained from Sue's face. Ellie reminded her quickly of their cover story and had her answer the phone. Sue's hand trembled as she said hello.

"Have you found our friend?" the man said over the phone.

Her voice wavering, Sue said, "Not yet. I called and got her service. I left her a message to call me immediately."

"*Liar!*" a scream echoed out of the phone.

"I swear I am telling the truth. I have not heard from her yet. Can I talk to my husband to know he is all right?"

"If you want to talk to your husband again, then you better get the answers to my questions and soon. Time is running out for your husband. I would hate to have to hurt him again if I find out you're lying!" Venom filling the man's voice.

"I swear I am not lying to you. Please don't hurt him. Please!" Sue's voice coming out in shallow cry.

"Let's hope you get the answers to my questions then." No emotion in the man's voice.

Click.

The line was dead.

Sue stared at the phone in her hand. Her body began to shudder and quake from the stress of the call. Her thoughts went to her husband. It was he that she would try to save from these madmen. If it took her last breath, Sue was determined to find Chuck and save his life!

Wanting to remain calm, Sue sat in the chair and said, "Let's get these sons of bitches!" Stress and anger, filling her voiced statement.

No one really said a word as they waited for darkness to descend over Montana. When it got dark enough, they all loaded into the SUV. Ellie was at the wheel with Sue in the front passenger seat. Shelby sat in the back, holding a shotgun and shells she had confiscated from the cabin.

Shelby examined the gun and hoped she would be able to remember how to use it. It looked much like the one her father had for hunting game birds in the wheat fields. It was a twenty-gauge pump action, and with a little finessing and fumbling of the bullets, she was able to load the weapon. Relief showing across her brow.

As Ellie, Sue, and Shelby were in the car and headed down toward Log Gulch Campground. From around the corner came Stacy and Lynn in Stacy's car. Shelby saw the car first and hit the floor boards. She had scared Sue and Ellie with her sudden throwing of her body to the floor. They both looked into the back seat. Both clearly thinking the girl had suddenly just lost her mind. Each giving the other a questioning look.

"Ellie. Didn't you recognize that car? It was Stacy and Lynn." Peeking her head up over the center column between the two front bucket seats.

"It was? I didn't even recognize them. I think we are fine. Remember my car was hidden behind the bushes, so I doubt they would know what we are driving." Uncertainty filling Ellie's voice.

Ellie gave a reassuring smile into the rearview mirror that was directed at Shelby. Hoping that both girls had been in contact

SAVA MATHOU

with Howard or Steve, Ellie tried to remember if she had seen any brake lights after the car had passed them. She hadn't thought so. Thankfully, they had passed them on a corner. Hopefully, Stacy's eyes had been on the road and not on the corner as she had rounded the curve.

Shelby got up from the floor of the Explorer and returned to her seat.

Looking in the rearview mirror, Ellie could see Shelby's confidence had begun to slowly disappear. Reaching back between the space between the bucket seats, Ellie patted Shelby's knee and gave her another award-winning grandmother smile. Seeing Shelby relax at her smile, Ellie focused back on the road. Ellie knew the girl had needed a little love and understanding.

Reaching the campground. All three began to look for a forest service road. They began to circle the campground. Not finding anything that lead off from the day parking lot, or in Little Log Gulch, they began to drive up into the main part of the campground.

Almost giving up, Sue spotted a silver gate as they rounded the corner that led up to the upper pavilion in the back of the park. Sue yelled for Ellie, "Stop the truck!" Ellie's foot hit the brake, bringing the tires to a halt with a chirp that turned some heads of some of the campers in that end of the park. Ellie gave the closest camper a defusing smile and a happy-go-lucky wave. The campers turned back to their fire. Ellie breathed a quick sigh of relief.

Backing up the vehicle, Sue said she was sure she saw a small road and gate beyond that last travel trailer. Turning her lights on high beams, the gate came into view as the vehicle came to a stop in the corner of the campground road. Ellie put the truck in drive and inched forward to the gate. Both women in the front seats must have seen the lock at the same time because they gave each a now-what look.

Sitting and staring at the gate for a moment, Ellie remembered the bolt cutter in the back of the SUV. She told Shelby to reach in back and grab the bolt cutter for her. Looking around the end of the camp ground, Ellie cut the lights only leaving on the parking lights. It looked like no one was at the last camper that was still plainly in view. She hoped no would wake up or come back to see what she was about to do. Her first felony: destroying government property. Ellie only gave it only a momentary thought. It needed to be done. She would deal with the consequences later.

Ellie got out of the truck with the bolt cutters in her hands. She walked nonchalantly over to the gate. Squinting to get a look at the lock, she placed the cutting edge of the tool onto the lock. Squeezing the handles together with all her strength, Ellie was only able to cut into the lock latch bar slightly. Summoning Shelby from the vehicle with a wave of her hand, Shelby moved quickly to Ellie's side. Ellie asked Shelby to help her pull together the handles of the bolt cutter because by herself, Ellie did not possess enough strength to cut the lock. Together, they strained to cut the bolt. With a snap, the bolt let loose and fell to the ground. Both women let out an audible sigh of relief.

Ellie climbed back into the John Sr.'s truck and put the truck in gear. Still leaving only the parking lights on, they both watched as Shelby opened the gate. As Ellie drove through, Sue rolled down her window and let Shelby know that she should close it behind them. Ellie pulled up out of the way of the gate and watched in the brake lights as Shelby closed the gate. Before going back to the vehicle, Shelby grabbed the broken lock on the ground and gave it a toss off into the bushes. Shelby hoped that by doing this, no one would get suspicious. She hoped.

Running back to the truck, Ellie had already in gear and pulled away as Shelby was still closing the rear door of the vehicle. Starting up the road, Ellie turned back on her lights and switched them to low beams. They had to see but no use having on the bright lights for everyone to see in the campground.

Traveling up the road, Ellie again watched the rearview mirror for any sign of being seen. Coming to the first creek crossing was easy. It was the second crossing that made them all jump and grab onto something close. Their journey across the second creek crossing was a bit of a ride. The middle of the creek at this point was wider. Ellie was unable to see in the dark that the middle of the channel was washed out. The front tires came to a jarring halt in the middle of the creek. On instinct, Ellie switched the truck in four-by-four low and stepped on the gas. The wheels spun and then grabbed on the gravel. The truck had picked up a little speed when the back tires hit the wash in the creek. All three women found themselves, flying in the air for a moment as the truck seat slammed back into their butts as the vehicle climbed out of the creek.

Breathless and shaken by the ride. All three sat in silence as Ellie continued guiding the vehicle up the road. Climbing a small hill, Ellie saw another creek crossing. The road crossing the creek tilted the vehicle on a slant, and all were holding on as they crossed the creek. This crossing had been much easier. Sue started to laugh, saying, "I had thought that crossing was going to be pretty wicked too!" Ellie and Shelby joined in on the laughter. Beside the slant of the vehicle from the hillside, the crossing had been much easier.

Coming out the creek bed, Ellie spotted a cattle gate up ahead that lead onto the ranch. Sue noticed that this gate was locked as well. She told Ellie to stay in the car and that she and Shelby would get this lock. Ellie, glad for the momentary reprieve, let the two younger women cut the luck. Both women slid the barbed wire gate open as Ellie drove their transport through the opening. They dragged the gate back across the road, and it took both women's strength to get the wire loop over the top of the post that held the wire gate closed.

The next mile-and-half of road was pretty easy for the most part. Except for a couple of good poles holes, it was pretty easygoing. Ellie stopped to check the map to try and see where they were located in proximity to the ranch. It wouldn't do any of them any good, if they just drove up to the front door and let everyone know they were there. Those consequences could be deadly.

Studying the map, Ellie thought she recognized their location. She let the other two know that it looked like they would have to drive up over the mountain. The ranch should be just over the mountain on the other side. They would have to drive up to the top of the rise so they would be able to see if the ranch was close on the other side. Hopefully, the ranch has some lights still on and would be able to show their distance from the main house and barn.

Switching the truck back into four-by-four low, Ellie slowly moved the truck forward and up the road that led to the top of the mountain. Her knuckles were white while grasping the steering wheel. She was glad it was dark so she couldn't see the drop off that lay next to the road. One wrong move, and it would be a bad bobsled ride back down the mountain. The wheels occasionally spun and grabbed for traction on the loose shale rock. Each time the wheels spun and reached for something to grip on, you could hear all three gasp and inhale quickly. None of them would really breathe again until reaching the safety of the top of the mountain.

Ellie's fingers began to loosen the grip she held on the steering wheel. Fresh blood, flowing back into her whitened fingertips. She was even able to let out a small sigh of relief.

That is until she saw what lie ahead.

Bringing the truck to a halt, what lay in front of them almost made her let out a string of swear words that would make a sailor blush. Instead, she reached into the center counsel and retrieved the flashlight that was stored there. Taking the flashlight with her, she exited the vehicle and switched on the light.

The handheld light showed her that she was just another step away from sliding down the mountain. Carefully, she made her way along the vehicle. Getting safely to the front of the vehicle, she made her way to the washout that stretched across the road in front of them. Staring down into it, she saw that it looked much more dangerous from the shadows that were cast by the headlights. The truck could make it over the wash, but it was going to be a bit bumpy and scary. The part of the wash, leading down the mountain on the outside would make the vehicle tilt, making for one heck of a ride, but they could make it. Hopefully, luck and angels were on their side this evening. Ellie knew they had to keep going.

Walking back to the car. She made her way along to the driver doors. Opening the door, the shale rock gravel beneath her left foot gave way. Her feet suddenly slipping out from under her, Ellie grasped for the steering wheel just moments before sliding down the mountainside. Grabbing for the steering wheel had saved her life.

Both Sue and Shelby let out a scream!

Together, both women reached for Ellie's hand and arm that were now wrapped around the steering wheel. Both women latched onto her with a death grip and pulled her into the vehicle with all their might. They were not about to let their friend slide down the mountain to her death. Pulling her into the cab, Ellie's faced was flushed and full of sweat as her body leaned back into the safety of the driver's seat.

Moments passed as Ellie regained her composure. Breathing deeply and trying not to think about how close she had come to death or serious injury, she told Sue and Shelby to get out of the vehicle. She would drive the SUV across the wash alone. If she was going to go down the mountain, it would be by herself, and she wasn't going to take her friends with her. It would be dangerous enough with one person. Let alone three.

Shelby was the first to speak up, "All for one, I guess. I am not leaving you, Ellie."

Sue made a sound of agreement, "Yep!"

Ellie simply said, "Then you both better put your seat belts on and hold on tight. This could get ugly." Knowing full well both were not leaving the vehicle or her.

Putting the truck into drive, Ellie looked one at a time at both women. Each nodded back to Ellie with a look of encouragement. Putting her foot on the gas, the SUV slowly moved forward into the wash. The nose of the vehicle dropped and dipped into the wash, and all three let out a scream. The front of the truck was leaning to the outside of the road and close to the mountain's edge.

Ellie gave the engine some gas as the lights of the vehicle began the climb up out of the wash. Just as the nose began to climb out, the rear of the truck began to slide down into the wash. The rear end was sliding on the loose shale because of the weight of the vehicle and the tilt of the road. Ellie sensed where the truck was heading. She knew this wasn't going to be good!

Her foot pushed the accelerator to the floor boards. The engine came roaring to life and gave the needed power to all four wheels. The tires started to spin and miraculously found some traction in the loose shale. The back driver's side wheel caught the edge of the mountain cliff side. Ellie could feel the truck, getting away from her. Instinctively, she turned into the slide, and the back wheel caught the road. The wheels' new traction brought them up out of the dangerous washout. It threw the truck back onto the narrow road. Ellie had to turn the steering wheel back quickly because now, the nose of the truck was headed off the mountain!

Luckily, there was a slight turn in the road that lead away from the mountain edge and back up the mountainside. The engine still roaring beneath them, Ellie brought the vehicle up the mountain and rode with quickness and an agility that even surprised her. Seeing a small level area, Ellie brought the truck to a quick stop, throwing them all forward.

Ellie let her head slowly sink to her hands and onto the steering wheel. Letting out a sigh of relief, she raised her head and looked at her passengers. Sue sat stone faced, looking straight ahead and out the front windshield. Ellie placed her hand on Sue's forearm and shook it slightly. It took a moment to bring Sue out of her shock. Sue's headed turned toward Ellie. No sound came out of Sue's mouth, only a small barely perceptible nod. Sue was shaken but would be just fine.

Letting go of Sue's forearm, Ellie turned to check on Shelby in the back seat. Not seeing her on the seat, Ellie swung her arm between the front seats. She grasped the air, searching for Shelby on the floor of the truck. Not finding her, Ellie let out a scared yell of Shelby's name, "*Shelby!*" Ellie looked frantically over at Sue. Sue could see that she hadn't been able to locate Shelby. Sue spun around quickly in her seat, the seat belt, catching and rubbing her shoulder raw. Sue called Shelby's name.

"*Shelby!*" Sue yelled with concern.

No answer.

Both women looked at each other with panic in their faces.

Something made a sound in the back of the truck.

"*Shh!*" Ellie said while grabbing Sue's hand.

Both women twisted in their seats again to hear any sound that might be coming from inside the vehicle or the outside.

First, a small sound of laughter. Sue and Ellie looked at each other, and Ellie called for Shelby again.

"Shelby?" Ellie said in a puzzled voice.

More laughter.

"Shelby?" Both women said together, both looking confused.

"It's me. I am all right. I must have been thrown out of my seat when we went over the wash. Felt like someone had put me on spin cycle! Not sure how I came out of my seatbelt," Shelby said with a touch of laughter in her response.

"Are you sure you're all right?" Sue said quickly.

"I am fine, but can one of you open the back door so I can climb out? Sorry, I didn't answer you right away, but I am kind of wedged in here. I think I was in shock as to where I landed. I was doing a mental inventory of my body to see if I was all right. I hope I didn't scare you. But if you don't mind me saying, 'Do you mind if we don't do that again?'" Shocked laughter coming from the back of the SUV.

Ellie and Sue both exited the truck and ran around to the back of the vehicle to open the door. Getting the door to open, all their provisions came tumbling out the back of the vehicle and landed onto the ground. Ellie grasped a leg. Sue grasped an arm. Pulling Shelby up, they helped steady her and get her on her feet. Grabbing Shelby by the shoulders, Ellie threw her arms around the girl. Sue then enveloped them both in her arms. Smiles spreading across all their faces. They were a team, and they were in this together.

They had all made it up the mountain with only a few bumps and bruises. It had been a close call on that wash. The three sat on the ground next to the truck and sipped on some water. It had been too close for comfort, and none of them were in a hurry to get back in the vehicle.

"Not bad driving for a grandma!" Sue said with a friendly punch to Ellie's arm.

"Give me a few more weeks, and I will really be ready for some off-road fun!" Ellie joked back.

"I don't know about the two of you, but do you mind if I just watch next time from the sidelines?" Shelby said with a laugh.

CHAPTER EIGHT

Deciding to leave the vehicle right where it was at for now, the three women had decided to walk the last fifty yards to the top of the mountain. No one was in a hurry to get back in the truck. Grabbing the flashlights, they headed off.

Topping the rise of the mountain, they quickly extinguished their lights. The vantage point gave them a great view over the ranch, and they could see Howard's place lit up with lights. The women stood silently, looking out at the distance to the ranch. They were still a good couple miles by road before they reached the place where the ranch house was located.

Ellie and the girls decided that Shelby and Sue would lead the vehicle down the mountain road by flashlight. This would be much better than advertising their position by having the headlights of the vehicle, broadcasting their exact location. They hoped that from so far away that no one would really take notice of any beams from a couple of small flashlights.

Ellie once again got behind the wheel of the truck and prayed she would *not* drive off the mountain. Hopefully, the girls would be able to see well enough to guide the SUV away from any danger. She was white knuckling the wheel as it began to move forward and down the mountainside toward the ranch. Opening the window, she decided a little fresh air would help her nervousness, hoping the cool air would keep her alert and focused to the task at hand.

Shelby was walking along the outside of the road was closest to the edge of the mountain. Sue took the inside lane and made her way along the safest part of the road. Both women tried to keep their flashlights pointed directly at the ground. Focusing on the track on the road, they cupped the end of their flashlights with their hands.

Not one of them wanted to be found on this road at night with nowhere to go but down. By cupping the flashlights, the two hoped this would also block more light from anyone's view.

Ellie drove the vehicle quite nervously in its lowest gear. She looked out the windshield. Barely able to make out what little light was coming from the flashlights, sweat was pouring down the inside of her arms. Thankfully, Shelby and Sue were taking their time and not losing Ellie on the mountain road. Ellie inched the vehicle down the road. It was all she could do to keep the vehicle on the road. Clouds had obscured the moon from view, and the night was very dark. Ellie knew this was a benefit to them and helped them not to be seen by a reflection from the moonlight. Sometimes the moon in Montana was so bright that it actually cast a shadow in the dead of night! Tonight was not one of those nights. Thank God.

The ride down was much easier and smoother than the ride up. Shelby and Sue once again climbed back into their seats in the vehicle. Ellie asked if they minded taking a quick break. She needed to catch her breath before proceeding. They still didn't know what they were going to do to rescue Chuck. They had only figured that they would sneak onto the ranch and look things over and go from the there. This was spur-of-the-moment decision-making adventure.

Before moving forward, Ellie took her pistol from her purse and put a fresh magazine full of bullets into the gun. Seeing this, Shelby gave the pump-action shotgun a pump and loaded a shell into the barrel. Shelby and Ellie both checked to make sure the safeties were on.

Ellie told them that they should all look for a good spot to park the vehicle when they were close enough to walk the rest of the way to the ranch. This way, they could walk the rest of the way on foot and not be seen as easily. Also, they would need the vehicle later for a quick escape.

A small hog's back ridge blocked their view of the ranch. Sue took the brightest flashlight they had and guided their way. She pointed the flashlight out the passenger window and lit the way down the road. Getting to the ridge, they all decided that it was best to walk from here.

It wasn't so much of a ridge but more of a small knoll. They had parked their ride behind a small grove of large chokecherry bushes that were growing along the creek. Ellie carefully turned the vehicle around and backed in their newly found hiding spot. She managed to get the vehicle pointed nose first back to the road. This way, she would be able to take off in any direction that they would need as their escape. Ellie had no doubt that they would definitely need to escape the upcoming situation with their lives.

All three trudged their way up the hill. Not one of them was breathing easy when they reached the top of the rise. Shelby found a big rock along the side of the road and plopped down with a thud. Ellie and Sue were less picky and copped a squat right there in the middle of the road. Ellie made a silent vow that she would start walking every day again and start up her karate lessons again to get into shape. Looking over at Shelby and Sue, Ellie thought to herself that she bet the girls were making a similar vow. A smile, raising to her lips. It gave Ellie comfort to have both women with her on this adventure.

Sue was the first to rise from her sitting position in the road. She was eager to find her husband safe and sound. Thoughts were crossing her mind of their wedding so many years ago. She had agreed to marry Chuck not really knowing if it was the right choice for her or not. Chuckling to herself, she could now see no other man in her life. It had been a rough beginning for them both. Looking back over the years in her mind, she found it amazing that how far they had both come in their life together. *What a wonderful life it has been*, she mused.

Coming back into the moment, Sue found Ellie and Shelby, looking at her. Both women were silently staring at their friend. No words had to be said because they both knew that Sue was thinking of her husband that was no in the hands of murderers. They let Sue have her moment to steal herself to the situation ahead.

Standing up and really taking in the view of the ranch, they were much closer than they thought they would be. The view from the mountaintop had been a bit deceiving, and all three were thankful now that they had parked the truck down below. The running engine would have been heard easily at the top of the knoll.

Ellie led the way down the road toward the barn. Flashlights were kept off and would not be turned on again. Only if it was emergency would they be used. They were now about a hundred yards from the house and about sixty yards from the barn. Ellie put her pocket binoculars up to her eyes and surveyed the surroundings up ahead.

Sue whispered, "Do you see Chuck?"

"No, but someone just passed the French doors by the porch on the side of the house. I couldn't tell if the person was inside or outside because it was so quick," Ellie said quietly.

"That's Howard's den. Steve put me in there the night I snuck out to the barn and saw that poor man killed," Shelby informed them.

Ellie looked back and nodded. Scanning the area for people, she could see shadows in the barn, moving around. The main doors at the end of the runway, leading out of the barn were wide open. Bright lights shined down out of the doorway. Ellie watched the doorway, hoping to see who was casting the shadows.

Tapping Ellie on the shoulder. Shelby whispered to her that there was a drainage ditch that led past the barn. They should be able to sneak along the bottom of the ditch to get a better view of the open barn doors.

Sue and Ellie followed Shelby off the road and toward the ditch. Reaching the ditch, they followed Shelby's lead as she got on her hands and knees and began to crawl along the bottom of the ditch. The bottom of the drainage ditch was cold and damp. In a couple of spots, the ditch had some standing water in it. The water was cool to the touch, and all three made pains not to cause a splash or noise that might give away their hidden position.

Ellie was following in the rear. It is strange how crazy thoughts would pop into one's head in the weirdest moments. At this moment, Ellie thought she would pay for all this crawling in the morning. Even while gardening, Ellie had to wear knee pads to save her knees. If she forgot her new protection, she would be stiff and sore the next day. She knew that after tonight, she would be achingly sore again.

Her next thought was wondering what her karate teacher would think of her crawling along the bottom of some wet ditch. This would amuse him, and it brought a smile to her face. Trying to banish the stupid thoughts from her mind, her head bumped right into Sue's butt. Looking up, she saw that Shelby was looking over the ditch toward the barn. Ellie followed suit and brought up the binoculars.

Sue stayed in the ditch, not wanting to peek over the edge. She was afraid she would see Chuck hurt or dead. Thank God that she was on her hands and knees because she knew she would fall over if still standing. Taking quiet deep breaths, Sue knew she needed to get it together. This was no time for her to be falling apart at the seams. If she couldn't, she would be no good at helping rescue the man she loved. Slowly, she inched her way up along Ellie to look over the edge of the man-made ditch.

Throwing a hand over her mouth, Sue tried very hard not to get up to run or scream. She found Ellie and Shelby each grabbing a shoulder and pulling her back into the ditch. Sue landed with a small splash in the soggy moss that covered the bottom of their hiding spot. Sue hoped that it was just ditch water and that she hadn't peed her pants. Every emotion in her body just barely contained beneath the surface of her skin.

Ellie brought her mouth close to Sue's ear and told her to stay quiet. It was important that they not be found if they were to save Chuck's life. It looked like they had roughed up Chuck but that he looked all right. She said that most head wounds always look worse than they really are because the blood vessels were close to the surface and tended to bleed more. Ellie added that they needed to stay quiet for Chuck's sake. If they were going to help him, then they couldn't be found. Again, stressing the point to Sue to make sure her friend understood the gravity of the situation.

Sue had a look of terror and fear in her eyes. Ellie hoped that she wouldn't have to give her friend a good slap across the face to bring her out of her fear. Ellie knew she couldn't blame her friend. If the roles were reversed Ellie would be reacting the same way.

Suddenly, Sue whispered, "I understand." And Ellie nodded back in agreement.

The three women again crawled back up to the edge of the ditch to peer over to look at the barns occupants. Chuck was sitting in the same chair that the informant had been killed in a few weeks before. His hands were duck taped to the bottom back of the chair, and his feet taped tightly against the chair legs. His chest was taped many times around the back of the chair. His hands had zip ties that held tightly around his wrists, and his hands looked blue from lack of circulation. His head drooped as if he were sleeping or knocked out cold. They all prayed he was not dead.

CHAPTER NINE

Chuck wasn't sleeping.

Chuck's mind was trying to process what had happened to him.

Chuck had been sweeping and mopping up the floor of the bookstore when he heard the back door open and close. Some regular customers used the back entrance because of the extra parking in the back of the building. Not thinking anything of it, Chuck continued to work.

A small noise sounded behind.

He was just about to look up and welcome the customer when everything went black. His limp body crashed to the floor with the sound of dead weight, hitting the floor boards. His head bounced as his body came into contact with the floor.

Chuck had come to in the back of a truck. He could tell it was that of truck bed by the ridges that were now imprinted into his back and arms that were tied behind him. It took him a moment to realize that the truck bed had a cover over it and that he wasn't blind. Struggling to move, his head and neck pounded with pain. A white hot pain, coursing through his body that so filled with pain, almost sending him back into the land of darkness and sleep. Hoping unconsciousness would save his mind from the reality of the torture, this relief would not come just now.

Finding that his hands and ankles were tightly secured, he tried to roll over onto his stomach. He thought that if nothing else, then he would be able to relieve some of the pressure and pain that were now pounding in his arms. Rolling over, Chuck let out a loud scream as fresh oxygenated blood rushed back into his arms. This fresh blood to his arms sent a new round of pain and shock through his body. Tears of pain stung his eyes and rolled down his cheeks.

Tasting blood in his mouth, it felt as though his jaw and teeth would need a good surgeon to ever be right again. The taste of the blood made his gag, and Chuck breathed deep through his nose to stop from throwing up. Looking down toward his feet, he could make out a faint light, coming from what he guessed was the tailgate of the truck.

Moving to his side, he tried to get a better look at the light that was poking through the darkness of his prison. Each wiggle and squirm brought him closer to the back of the truck. With each move, pain wracked his body. Hoping to see out the crack that was bringing in light, his hopes were dashed as the darkness was playing tricks with his eyes. His eyes had adjusted to the dark and now looking at the light brought pain to his eyes. His pupils could not adjust between the darkness and light.

Pushing himself with his feet and legs, he found the wheel well with his head. This was a good resting spot until the moving vehicle hit a hole in the road. The jarring pain sent Chuck back into the darkness of being knocked out cold.

Awakened again.

Chuck now found himself now taped quite tightly to a chair. Taking in his surroundings, he realized he was in a horse barn somewhere. Looking around the room, his eyes tried to find something that could help him cut the tape. Not seeing anything, Chuck let his head drop and began to wonder what he had done to be put in this situation. Silently, Chuck began to say a prayer.

He was lost in thought when he heard a voice come from behind. Trying to quickly turn to see who was speaking, the pain almost caused him to vomit. White hot lights flashed danced in his eyes. It took a few minutes for his vision to clear and catch his breath. Not turning his head again, he heard a man speaking.

"Looks like our sleeping beauty has awakened from his nap!" The man's tone was selfish and cruel.

"I think your right there, boss! Do you think he wants to sit up and have a talk with us now?" Another voice sounded behind him.

Two men. Chuck realized.

"What do you want with me? I have not done anything to you. I don't even know who you are. I don't even recognize your voices." Chuck tried to reason with the still unseen men.

The two men came around to the front of Chuck so he could see who his attackers were. Not recognizing either man, he looked up at them with a questioning look on his face. Seeing the quizzical look on Chuck's face, both men began to laugh at him.

"It seems your bitch wife decided to help that nosey friend of hers and hide a girl that we want to find," Howard spoke with a frustration in his voice.

Ellie.

Chuck realized he was in serious trouble.

"A little birdie told us you all are good friends and that we might be able to trade your life for hers," Steve chimed in.

Shooting Steve a look.

Howard said, "Shut up, Steve!"

Steve. At least now, Chuck knew one of the men's names.

Howard spoke. "Seems your friend Ellie is a bit more resourceful than we gave her credit."

A smile crept onto Chuck's face. That was Ellie all right. He had known her for years and never knew what she was going to do next.

"I would wipe that smile off your face. Or we would be glad to take it off for you!" Steve's voice now cold.

"We don't know where Ellie is. She only stopped by to say that she would be out, working on a case and that she would get a hold of us when she got back," said Chuck. Fear rising on his vocal cords.

"See, now that is where you're wrong," Howard said simply.

"What do you mean?" Chuck asked.

"Looks like Ellie called your wife and asked her to bring her some supplies. Now it's just a waiting game for Ellie to contact your wife and let her know where to bring the food."

"How do you know that?" Chuck said confused.

"Like my friend here said earlier, a little birdie let us know after Ellie contacted him." Howard laughed as though his comment was funny.

Again, Howard spoke, "We are going to leave you now and call that ugly woman you call a wife. Let's hope for your sake that she has the answer we want!"

At that comment, the two men turned around and left Chuck alone in the barn. Chuck could hear Steve ask Howard what they were going to do if the wife didn't come through with the info they needed. Now he had both their names.

Howard and Steve.

Who was the third man that was giving them information about Ellie?

Chuck couldn't think of anyone that would want to sell Ellie out. Unless that person was somehow involved in whatever this was that he was now in. Chuck found himself very tired and tried hard not to fall asleep. Sleep overtook him quickly. His body was simply responding to the stress it had been put under in the last few hours.

Waking up to a sharp pain, searing across his face, Chuck realized that the man called Steve had just hit him across the face. His cheek was exploding with pain. His eyes filled with flashes of blinding light caused from the pain. Trying to get his focus back, he tried to right his vision by focusing on his aggressor's face. The blurred vision he was experiencing began to come back to normal. He found himself, looking up into the faces of two men who wanted to kill him. Their eyes cold and dark. The faces of two men who had lost what little of their souls they once may have had. It was clear now that there was no human emotion at all in their eyes. They were the faces of men who had killed without remorse or compassion.

"Either your wife is lying to us, or Ellie hasn't got back into contact with her yet. So we are going to find out if you are lying to us too," Howard said while raising a bat and striking Chuck's ribs.

The wind flew out of Chuck as he felt the bat strike the bone of his ribs. He heard the sickening crack of a rib, breaking under the pressure of the blow. His breathing coming in irregular bursts.

"I don't know anything. I swear!" Chuck cried in vain for them believe him.

"Why is it that I am having trouble believing you?" asked Steve.

"Maybe this will change your mind!" Howard said.

Taking the bat in his hand again. Howard swung the bat at the man's legs. A sickening perverted look coming across his face. He was enjoying causing the man pain and misery. Howard continued to work over the fleshy area of the man's thighs, being careful not to kill the man but made sure he was feeling every bit of the pain. Steve steadied the man's shoulders to keep him from falling over backward from the hits to his legs.

Screaming out, Chuck yelled! "Please. I don't know anything! I swear! Sue and I have not spoken since this morning. She had been out on some errands for the store. I swear!"

With that last plea, Chuck fell off into a sleep caused by the amount of pain his body was being forced to endure.

A sharp searing pain in the ribs woke him to again face the men who were now his enemies. His ribs were on fire. Breathing was not coming easy to him. Trying to catch his breath, pain shot through his body, making it impossible to even lift his head without pain. His voice now coming in a raspy whisper.

"What? I don't know anything. Please. You have got to believe me."

The men had to bend over to hear the hoarse and quiet whisper that was now coming from their captive. Looking at each other, they both looked to believe the man's quiet statement of innocence.

*****

Chuck sat for hours in the chair after his tormenters left him. He wept from the pain. Trying to choke back a sob that shook his body with fresh new pain, he fought to catch his breath and calm himself. His body felt like it had been hit by a large truck, and they had stopped and ran over him again and again.

His thoughts drifted to Sue and the kind smile that always graced her lips. Her face brought him a calm that he desperately needed now. He hoped that she would remain safe. If he knew Sue, she was out there somewhere, hatching up a plan with Ellie. If he was lucky, then she had contacted the police, and they had a search underway for him now. He would just have to remain strong and hope they found him soon. Chuck needed and wanted a hospital, and the best pain medication that they could pump into his body.

Night had fallen, and the two men still hadn't returned. His ears were straining for any sound that would help him know where they were lurking. Occasionally, Chuck thought he heard the sound of a television. A house had to be nearby. He also kept hearing what sounded like the squishing of water. His thoughts went to a creek, or some water source nearby.

Chuck fought off sleep but thought a little rest couldn't hurt. The men hadn't come back, and he could use a little sleep. He needed every ounce of strength he could get if he was going to survive.

Splash.

Chuck heard the water splash and wondered what it could be. Probably just some deer or animals from the ranch. His mind drifting back to sleep.

CHAPTER TEN

Yelling was now coming from the house. All three women watched the windows and strained to hear the argument from within the walls of the ranch home.

Sue and Ellie were making a great effort to listen to the agitated voices when they realized Shelby was no longer with them. Looking around and searching for their companion in the dark, they saw her, sneaking up to the edge of the barn. Shelby was staying to the shadows and quiet as a mouse in her movements. Both Ellie and Sue looked at one another with each having a mouth that agape in awe.

Ellie felt her blood pressure rise even more as she watched Shelby move across the darkness. The girl hadn't even said a word. She just took off and now was probably going to get herself killed. Ellie silently applauded the girl for her bravery as well. Foolish but brave. Her eyes continued to follow the girl as she reached the main doors.

Shelby thought to herself, *I am not going to let this man die because of me.* Looking over at Ellie and Sue, she saw their attention was being held by the goings on of the house. This was her chance to sneak off and try to free Chuck. Quietly, she sunk back down into the ditch. Getting to her feet and ducking down, she ran off along the drainage. The ditch brought her closer to the barn.

Leaving the safety of her hiding place, she left the ditch at a run. Making sure to stay in the shadows, she hoped that no one remained in the barn with Chuck. Moving along the wall of the barn, Shelby crept up to the main doors of the barn. The lights prevented her from entering the doors and getting to Chuck's side. Anyone watching the barn from the house would be able to spot her the moment she stepped out into the light.

Retracing her steps along the wall of the barn, she remembered she had entered the barn by a side barn stall door. Hoping one still remained open, she moved around the corner of the barn, trying to see where she was going. The darkness was playing tricks with her eyes.

Shelby walked right into the wire of an electric fence. The shock of electricity almost made her yelp out in a sudden burst of surprise. Her muscles were involuntarily contracting from the electrical shock. Getting back her senses quickly, she ducked quickly under the wire. She spotted an open door up ahead.

She was sneaking quietly up to the open stall door. Her hearing was at full attention for any hidden foe that may be waiting to kill her. All her senses were on full alert. Shelby stuck her head out to peek into the open doorway. Seeing that the way was clear, Shelby entered the barn. Silently, she moved across the vacant horse stall.

Looking carefully through the slats of the stall's boarded wall, she looked around the barn to make sure no one else was also hiding in the darkness. Quietly, she opened the latch of the stall door. Shelby crept out.

The squeaking of the hinges made Chuck lift his head slightly to find the approaching noise. Raising his eyes to follow the noise. He saw a girl, sneaking toward his direction. His first thought was that of being saved by an angel.

Tiptoeing up to the man that she was here to save, Shelby whispered that she was here to help get him out of here. She let Chuck know that Sue and Ellie were waiting outside for them. Grabbing the knife from her pocket, Shelby began to cut away the many layers of duct tape that kept Chuck fastened to the chair.

With each pull of the sticky tape being removed from his body, Chuck fought the urge to scream. His grunts of pain came out with heavy exhalations of breath. He tried his best to remain silent as the girl removed the tape from him.

Looking into the man's face, Shelby felt a pity for the man. He was obviously in pain and with each layer of tape cut brought him more pain. Tears slid down her cheeks as she did her best not to cause him anymore pain than he was already in. She could tell he was doing his best not to scream out. Cutting the tape from his elbows, he let out a cry of relief and pain. Looking at the zip ties on his wrist, Howard and Steve had no care when they put the tight ties on Chuck's wrists. Both hands were blue from lack of circulation. The plastic was so tight against the skin, and Shelby was afraid that she might cut his skin in releasing him from his bonds.

Slowly, she turned the knife so the back dull edge was against his skin. Pushing the point of the blade under the tight plastic binds brought blood to the surface of his skin as well. Sucking in her breath, she held it in as she pushed the metal further.

The first band cut quickly.

She examined the cut and saw that it was shallow and barely a scrape. Thankfully, his hands had no feeling from the lack of circulation. She again slid the knife up under the other band on his wrist. This one was much tighter, and more blood was shown on the blade. It was now or never. Pulling the knife upward, the plastic band cut free.

Grabbing his arm, she hoisted Chuck from the chair. Chuck could not suppress the yelp of pain that escaped his lips. Shelby and Chuck stood silently for any noise or footsteps, coming from the ranch house. Chuck's body did not want to cooperate with Shelby's movements. The man was barely able to stand, let alone walk. She gently sat Chuck back into the chair. She knew she would need something to help move Chuck. Looking around, she saw a wheelbarrow.

Running to get the wheelbarrow, Shelby brought the wheelbarrow back over to Chuck. Placing his legs between the handles of the implement, she helped Chuck to his feet. Turning him around, she lowered him into the wheelbarrow. Shelby wasn't going to be able to carry him, so she would push him out. She would be able to move him much faster by pushing the wheelbarrow than trying to carry him out.

She opened the door of the stall that she had used to come into the barn. Pushing Chuck into the stall, she set the wheelbarrow and Chuck back down. She had seen a saddle blanket, hanging over another stall. Quickly grabbing the saddle blanket. Shelby dragged the saddle blanket over the ground. Shelby hoped this would obscure any tracks they may have left in the barn. She wasn't going to be able to rid the ground completely of their tracks. However, this just might throw them off track a little bit, long enough for them to get away.

Taking the saddle blanket with her into the stall, she lifted Chuck's head and placed the blanket between his head and the metal. The blanket might provide a little cushion and some added comfort. Looking down at Chuck's face, she didn't believe any more damage could be done to a man, but she didn't want to risk it. This would provide some comfort over the bumps of the fields they would have to traverse to get back to the truck.

Reaching for the handles of the wheelbarrow, Shelby began to push the wheelbarrow out of the barn. They ran into their first obstacle quickly. There was a cement foundation that ran along the base of the barn. It also happened to run across the bottom of the stall darn that led to the outside paddock. It stuck out a couple inches above the dirt, knowing she could get him over it, but the pain was going to be immense. Letting Chuck know of what was about to happen, Chuck gave a grunt and a nod of understanding. He had tried to speak, but it came out in a raspy whisper, and she couldn't understand what he said. Thinking it would be best to get it over quickly, she gave a quick push. The wheelbarrow bounced and jarred poor Chuck. His scream was almost more than she could bare. Thankfully, it wasn't a loud scream, but anyone within a short distance could have heard it. Whispering in Chuck's ear, Shelby let him know to stay as quiet as possible. Howard and Steve were only a short distance away in the house.

Heading off again with her human cargo, Shelby had visions of what a Sherpa must feel like trying to carry heavy loads up Mount Everest. Grabbing the electric fence wire with her bare hands, Shelby fought the pain of the shock and quickly wheeled Chuck under the wire to safety. Her neck muscles were in spasm. She had placed the electric wire on the back of her neck to keep it from touching Chuck, trying to protect his now-fragile body from the electricity that surged through the wire.

Ellie and Sue saw Chuck and Shelby reach the edge of the drainage ditch. Quickly, Ellie and Sue grabbed the front of the wheelbarrow to help Shelby get Chuck to the other side. It would take all three to get across the man-made ditch.

As they got Chuck to the bottom of the ditch, their faces all blanched as they heard a yell come from the barn.

"Howard! He is gone! *Howard*!" Steve's voice tore through the night.

From the house. "What the hell are you yelling about out there? You want everyone to hear you?" Howard replied.

"I said he is gone!"

Hearing this, Howard flew from the porch, running to the barn. He came to a sliding halt in the front entrance to the barn. Seeing the empty bloody chair, he punched the wall and swore out into the night.

"I know you fucking bitches are here! You had better hope I don't find you because when I do, I am going to take my time killing all of you. By the time I am done, you're going to praying for death to come and take you!" Howard's animalistic voice shook the darkness.

The women sat in the bottom of the drainage ditch with Chuck still lying still in the wheelbarrow. Ellie drew the pistol from the waistband of her jeans. Taking off the safety, she hoped that she would not have to use the weapon. She would not enjoy having to kill a man but would not hesitate to protect her client or Chuck and Sue with her life.

Looking over, Ellie saw Sue, stroking Chuck's hair and planting quiet kisses on his better and less-bruised cheek. Seeing the state of her best friends, Chuck lay in a prone position in the wheelbarrow. Ellie said a quick prayer for him to survive. A fire rose in her belly. It angered her that those men could be so filled with hate that they had no remorse in destroying or taking a life.

Looking over the edge of the mound, she saw both men run to the vehicle that had tried to run them off the road. The truck spun around. The headlights, showing right over their hiding spot for a brief moment. Ellie threw her head to the ground in response to the lights, hitting her head on rock. *Great*, she thought. *Knock myself out before we can even get away.*

Seeing the truck head back down the road away from their direction, the women didn't waste any time, grabbing the wheelbarrow and lifting it out of the ditch. Ellie pointed Shelby and Sue toward the truck and told them to get moving. Sue and Shelby both stopped.

"You're not coming with us?" Sue asked.

"I am going to get into that house and find some evidence," Ellie replied.

"*You're what?* Ellie, let's just get out of here now!" Sue yelled.

"You know as well as I that this will never be over without any evidence. If they have someone, helping them from the police, then we are going to need something good on them to put them away." Ellie was talking to herself as much as them.

Sue reached out for Ellie and pulled her tight to her. They looked into each other's eyes. No words were said. The two friends knew each other so well that words were not needed. Neither could have come up with any even if they had wanted too.

Shelby came around the wheelbarrow and hugged Ellie. Tears sliding down the pink of her cheeks. Ellie brought her hand to Shelby's face and wiped away the tears. Once again, Ellie gave Shelby her best loving grandmotherly smile.

"Go. Get Chuck into the Explorer. Make sure you get him as comfortable as you can. Don't put him in the back laying down. Seat him the back seat. It's going to be a bumpy ride back over that mountain. The seat will give him some cushion for the ride. If I am not there in exactly one-half hour, you need to promise that you will leave and go get some help." Ellie would not let them go until they promised.

Ellie kissed them both on the cheek and bent down and kissed Chuck lightly on the forehead. Looking at his eyes, she could see a slight smile come to his face. His hand, reaching up to grasp hers in his. He gave her a barely perceptible squeeze of his hand and then his arm fell back into the wheelbarrow. Ellie looked upon her friend with a smile. It must have taken all his strength to lift that hand.

Watching the two-wheel Chuck over the rugged terrain, her heart reached out to him because it was going to be a difficult and painful ride for him back to the truck. At least, they could get back to the truck and relative safety of the vehicle. She stood there, watching them go until they descended down the hill toward the creek.

Turning around, she faced the house. Taking a deep breath, she realized that she had no idea what she was looking for. Surveying the road, she watched for lights and listened for the sound of a vehicle. Hearing no sounds except those of frogs and seeing no lights, she took off at a fast pace for the house. Forgetting about the ditch, Ellie had almost gone headfirst into the ditch. Sliding across the rough gravel on her bum, Ellie let out a cuss.

"Damn! Guess this will be just one more bruise to add to the collection. My body is going to look like an inkblot test gone bad."

Realizing that she was wasting time, Ellie climbed to her feet and brushed off the dust and bits of gravel from her jeans. Seeing and feeling that she was fine, Ellie climbed out of the ditch. Carrying the pistol in her hand, Ellie was being careful not to be seen by anyone that may be lurking still on the property. They had only seen Howard and Steve but that didn't mean that someone hadn't stayed behind to be a look out or surprise them.

Ellie had almost reached the steps of the large ranch house when she heard a groan coming from her left toward the barn. Not breathing, she strained to hear where the sound had been coming from. Ellie let out her breath with a swoosh of air.

Reaching the stairs of the side porch, Ellie heard another distinct groan. This time, she knew her ears and mind were not playing tricks on her. It had the definite sound of a person who was hurt or in trouble. Turning on her heels, Ellie made her way toward the sound of the groans for help. Coming up on the side of the barn that faced the house, she could see a side door open. Tiptoeing up to the side barn stall door, Ellie stood silently just outside the door. Her mind racing and hoping that this wasn't a trap. Taking the small flashlight from her pants pocket, she bravely switched on the light.

Hoping the bright light of the LEDs would blind her would-be attacker. Ellie stuck out her hand and shined the light into the stall. Stealing herself for an attack, Ellie slowly peeked around the edge of the door into the stall. Looking around the stall, Ellie found Officer Jim Barkley tied on the ground. His eyes were squinting in the bright light. Ellie quickly moved the light to survey the rest of his body.

Silver duct tape bound his ankles and his hands behind his back. A patch of tape was covering his mouth.

Ellie ran to his side. Quickly removing the tape from his mouth, Jim let out a shrill cry as the sticky gag was removed from his lips. His voice was dry and hoarse when he spoke.

"Ellie. Thank God! They have my daughter. You need to get her out of the house!" The fear of a caring father, filling his words.

"Jim. We thought… I thought that you were the one, helping them and the one in charge of them?" Ellie asked.

"I am. I was. But not how you think. They have been holding my daughter so that I would be forced to help them." Shame in Jim's voice.

CHAPTER ELEVEN

Stress and worry filled Jim's words as he began to tell Ellie what happened. Ellie undid his binds as he began his story.

"I was working with the task force for the last year to a year and a half. Apparently, I kept getting too close to them.

"One day, I had come across one of their meth labs up in the Stickney Creek area. I was by myself that day. I just happened to be out on patrol and had gotten a tip. I decided to check it out on my own. Most tips are bogus or are people just trying to be vengeful to someone and usually don't amount to anything."

"This day it was a trap. The tip that I received was from them. Howard and Steve. They had wanted me to find the lab and come there. I was just about to radio in my find, when Howard stepped out of the trailer that housed the drugs. He walked out of the trailer and had a smug look on his face."

Jim continued.

"I had my weapon drawn on him, and he had this big smile on his face like all was well with the world. He told me to put down the gun and that he and I needed to talk. I remember thinking, *What could you and I have to talk about?*

"Anyway, he proceeded to tell me that he had my daughter and that he would be keeping her safe and hidden until I could make a problem go away for him. He had one of those little portable DVD/TV players with the small television screen. You know, the ones that look like a miniature laptop computer. Pressing play, my daughter came on the screen and was tied to a chair. She was crying and screaming for me to help her."

The look of a man thoroughly defeated. Jim spoke again.

"For God's sake. She is only ten years old, and the animals have her tied up in a chair. You could hear them taunting her to cry out for her daddy!

"I was so angry. I almost shot the man right there. He could see that I was ready to kill him. Seeing this, he told that if I ever wanted to see my daughter alive again, I was going to have to play ball and help them out."

Anger filling Jim's face and voice.

"They found out that I wasn't really helping them out but stringing them along until I could find my daughter."

Ellie nodded and continued to listen to Jim.

"I got out here tonight, realizing that this was the only place I have not checked yet. Knowing that my daughter was here, I came out ready to settle the score with those two.

"They were ready for me. Someone else is helping them out because they knew I was coming. I still don't know how or who. They plan on using me for the fall guy. I am not sure what they are planning yet.

"We have to get my daughter out of that house and to safety."

Ellie replied. "Jim, let's go get your daughter."

A smile came across in her voice and spreading across her face. She was happy to find out that it wasn't Jim that had set her up. There would be a lot more question later, but for now, they had to get his daughter back. Ellie asked if Jim was fine to walk.

Searching the fields and road that lay outside the stall door, Ellie again found herself, searching for lights and the noises of a car engine. They made their way to the steps of the house. Ellie was feeling a sense of repeating herself. Coming to the French doors of the porch, Jim eased the door open. Ellie stood behind him with her pistol drawn, feeling a bit like Clint Eastwood. Ellie was ready for this night to be over. She got the feeling that the night was just beginning.

Entering the house, they found it empty. No one had been left behind to protect Howard's stronghold. They decided to split up. It would be much faster to search the house separate than together.

Ellie began her search of the bedrooms. Coming up with nothing, she met Jim back in the living room in the main part of the house. Ellie sat back on the sofa. The cushions felt so good beneath. She had to will herself to keep moving, or she would fall asleep right there on the sofa.

Waiting for Jim to finish searching the kitchen and mud room, Ellie again heard a noise. Yelling for Jim, Jim came to the living room. A look of questioning crossed his face. She held her eyes on him with her pointer finger of her hand held up. That international symbol to stop and be very quiet.

Jim stopped immediately and was quiet as a church mouse. His head shifted and turned on the room, scanning it for any noise, or something he may have missed.

"The basement!" he almost yelled.

Jim turned quickly and was at the door in the mud room that led to the basement. Ellie could hear his footsteps descend the stairs. They had the sound of a man on a mission. Ellie still remained standing at the sofa. She didn't think the noise was coming from the basement. It was too easy of a hiding place.

Returning from his search of the basement, Jim had a look of despair on his face. Ellie knew loss, but she couldn't begin to imagine the loss of a child. It was against nature for a parent to lose a child. A child was meant to lose a parent sooner or later but not the other way around. Her heart ached for the desperate man who stood before her.

Walking to where the hallway met the living room, Ellie looked from the hallway to the living room and back a few times. Jim knew she had found something and stayed silent, letting her figure out whatever she was putting together in her mind. Ellie knew something wasn't right about the layout of the house.

"Jim, can you come here for a moment?" asked Ellie, still looking from the living room to the hallway and back again.

"What have you got, Ellie?" Jim trying to see what Ellie was wanting to find.

"Something is *not* right about this room! I think there is a secret room. Look at the hall and then look at the living room, and you will see that it doesn't add up. Stand here and tell me what you see." Ellie moved aside for Jim to look from her previous vantage point.

"Ellie, I am afraid I just see a hall and a living room."

"Look again. See that door on the right down the hall? That's a bathroom. It is a small bathroom too! There is no way it comes all the way down the hall to back up to the living room. There has got to be a good twelve feet from that bathroom wall and the wall of the living room," she said.

Jim went down the hall. Switching on the bathroom light, he scanned the bathroom, looking at Ellie and then looking into the bathroom again.

"You're right," was all he said. Jim's mind now realizing what Ellie was talking about. The rooms and walls didn't make sense.

Jim began moving down the hall, pressing against the wall and moving things on the shelves in the hall. It dawned on Ellie that he was looking for an entrance into the room. Ellie joined the search in the hall. Finding nothing that would allow them entrance into the room, Ellie shrugged her shoulders at Jim. They moved to the living room.

Again, both began to search.

Ellie just happen to notice a scratch on the floor in front of the rug. She would have never seen it. Jim must have flipped up the rug with his foot when he crossed the living room to her in the hall. Pulling back the rug, the scratch went in an arch shape. Following the arch over toward the wall, it looked like the entertainment center pulled out. Getting Jim's attention, she pointed out what she had found.

Seeing what she had found, immediately, Jim began to pull at the entertainment center. It moved ever so slightly but did not move forward. His frustration and fear and anger were giving him momentum. Jim grabbed the back of the entertainment center and gave a huge jerk to the console.

The sound of wood, splitting and cracking filled the air. Ellie grinned when Jim looked back at her. Giving it one last jerk, the latch holding the entertainment center to the wall broke loose. With that, the piece of furniture moved out easily in an arch motion. The right side of the entertainment center was on a hinge!

Bringing her flashlight out again and handing it to Jim. Jim switched it on and moved closer to shine the light into the dark room. In the corner on a small bed, Jim saw his little girl curled up in the fetal position. Jim moved quickly over to the bed. Ellie had followed Jim into the room and remained silent in the background.

Jim sat down on the edge of the bed and reached out his arm toward his little girl. Touching her shoulder, the girl pulled back and screamed. Jim began to shush her and let her know it was her dad and that he was there to rescue her. Her eyes slowly opened and looked at the man in front of her. The look on her face was one of confusion. Lifting her head from the pillow, she spoke, "Daddy?"

"It's me, honey. Ms. Ellie and I are here to get you out of here. It's going to be all right." The love filling his words.

"Oh, Daddy. It really is you!" Tears filling the little girl's eyes. Rubbing her eyes, she jumped up from the bed and rushed into her father's arms.

Ellie found herself at a loss for words. Tears streaming down her own cheeks.

"Melissa, we need to get going. We can't stay here. There are some bad men, and we need to get going," Jim let her know.

Ellie walked over to the bed, reaching out her hand.

"Hi, Melissa. I am Ellie. Your dad grew up with my son, John Jr. Your daddy and I are here to get you back home. Would you like that?" Her smile, shining bright at the young girl.

The little girl looked up and shook her head yes, then quickly buried her head back into her father's neck.

Jim scooped his daughter up into his arms and held her tight as all three exited her prison. They made their way back to the den and just reached the French doors that led to the deck when they saw lights, coming up the driveway. Ellie grabbed Jim's arm to stop him from walking out onto the deck. She moved her head to signal the lights, coming up the road. Seeing the lights, Jim told Melissa, "You need to be very quiet so the bad men will not find us. We need to be very quiet so that we can get away to Ms. Ellie's car."

Melissa simply nodded her head and then buried her face back into the protection of her father's embrace.

Ellie moved Jim behind her and watched as the truck approached the house. She could see Steve and Howard exit the truck. Her stomach lurched inside her, hoping they wouldn't come in through the side entrance where the three were now located. Watching them head toward the front door, she reached back and grabbed Jim by the elbow, and they moved quietly out onto the small deck. Closing the door with great care, Ellie pointed toward the drainage ditch. Seeing where Ellie was pointed, Jim moved off toward the ditch with Melissa still in his arms. Following up the rear, Ellie held the gun in her shaking hands as she watched for movement from the den.

Seeing a light come on in the den and a man move quickly to the French doors, thinking quickly, Ellie gave Jim and Melissa a quick shove that propelled them into the ditch and jumped down behind them. Hoping that the dark had hidden them well enough, Ellie whispered to Jim to stay down.

Steve had moved out onto the porch and was searching the darkened yard for signs of the intruders. In his hand, he held a pistol tight in his grip. Not seeing anyone in the yard, he fired several rounds into the air in frustration.

Reflex took Ellie by surprise, and she found herself, sliding down the ditch to duck the bullets. Looking at Jim and Melissa, she signaled them to move down the ditch. Slowly, they began their flight from the murderous Steve and Howard.

At one point, Melissa said, "Daddy, you're squeezing me too hard!"

Jim looked down at his daughter and apologized. He was nervous and wanted his daughter as far away from these men as possible. He had gathered Melissa to his chest when the gunshots were fired. In his response to protect his child, Jim didn't realize how tight he had been squeezing Melissa in his arms. Loosening his grip slightly, it would be a long time before he really let his daughter go. It had been too close a call for him, and he never again wanted to let his daughter out of his sight.

Looking down at his daughter, he saw the face of his wife, Lisa. It was amazing how much Melissa looked like her. He realized he hadn't really noticed this before. People would comment on the likeness, and he would nod. He noticed his mother in his daughter as well. It was amazing that moments like this made a person think and realize what is truly important in life. Smiling down at Melissa, he squeezed her tight and gave her a kiss to the top of the head. Melissa was young, but in moments like this, she was wise beyond her years. Hugging her father back and looking up at him, she said, "I love you, Daddy."

Ellie watched the two exchange words that didn't need to be spoken.

She understood the love of a parent for their child. She knew it in both of her children. It melted her heart to watch the tender moment. It had been a close call in the farm house, and they had gotten Melissa out just in time with only moments to spare.

Ellie looked up and over the bank to see if Steve was still on the deck. Not seeing anyone, she placed her hand on Jim's back, urging him forward. Realizing that it's easy to get caught up in a moment like this, but knowing it was time to keep moving forward because danger was still not far away, she tenderly moved Jim and Melissa forward toward the truck.

They had just begun to move again and had almost reached the mountain road, leading back down to the where the truck was hidden. Ellie and Jim both heard the distinct sound of gun metal click behind them. Someone had cocked a gun. The noise was unmistakable. A chill ran down their spines.

The three turned around to find Steve, pointing a pistol at them. Ellie, without thinking, naturally stepped in front of Jim and Melissa. Not really realizing what she had done. It was a simple mother's instinct to protect a child. This was now her battle. It was because of her case that everyone was involved. She would be damned if this maniac would hurt this little girl any more than he already had.

"So you all thought you could get away, huh?" Steve said with a smile of a predator smeared across his face.

"Let them go. You can take me. They are not involved in this," Ellie tried to reason with him.

"They are all plenty involved now. Looks like this ditch is going to be your grave." Steve was emotionless in response.

"Let my daughter go. She is innocent in all of this," Jim pleaded.

"Do I look like I care about your daughter? Shut up and show your daughter how to die like a man!" Steve replied with a voice full of contempt.

Ellie, knowing he was about to fire the weapon upon them, raised her pistol like a modern-day gunfighter and fired at Steve. Firing too quickly, her bullet still found its mark just a little lower than expected, hitting Steve in the upper thigh just below his groin. Ellie could see the blood stain, filling his pant leg and groin area.

In reaction to the gunshot wound, Steve dropped his gun and grabbed his leg and groin. His cry of pain pierced the night air. Falling to the ground and curling up in the fetal position, he was sliding back his head against the dirt and gravel on the ground.

His eyes met Ellie's.

"You fucking bitch. You shot me!" Surprise and hatred filling his words.

Ellie found a smile, coming across her face. She was cold in her response back to Steve. "You were going to kill us, and you're surprised I shot you? Get real. From my point of view, you deserve to die for what you have done."

She continued.

"Make one move, and I will treat you to some more lead! Where is your friend?"

He gave up no response.

"Young man, I suggest you answer my question." Ellie cocked the gun and pointed it at his groin again.

"You're all dead. You will never get off this ranch alive." Smiling at them, Steve thought he could scare them.

Pointing her gun at his knee, Ellie fired the pistol again, blowing his kneecap away. She looked down at the man. He was now on the verge of passing out. Grabbing his good leg, she pulled Steve down into the drainage ditch with them. Ellie never knew she could be angry enough to shoot a man. Quickly, she realized it was something that would never leave her mind again. It was not something she enjoyed, but it was a necessity to help save their lives. It was kill or be killed.

Might be good to have their own hostage, she thought.

She was checking over his wounds to make sure she hadn't hit an artery. He was scum to her, but she didn't want to see him die. It surprised her that she didn't. He had caused the people she cared about a great deal of pain and suffering. Ellie felt like a mother grizzly, protecting her young. Her heart was kind and full of love, but she would fight to the death for those she cared about.

Turning around to face Jim. She told him to get moving and head to the truck. Coming close to his ear, she whispered the location and the hiding spot of the vehicle and told him to get moving.

Now realizing this needed to end, she was going to find Howard and take him alive or not.

Before leaving the ditch, she checked Steve's pulse and his breathing to make sure he was all right. She felt no remorse about him, spending the rest of his life, recuperating in jail. He deserved a barred vacation in a nice gray cell. Ellie quickly refilled the gun clip and put it back in her gun. No sense in running out of bullets when she may need each and every one. Putting one into the chamber for good measure, Ellie began to climb out of the ditch toward the house.

She was just getting to the lip of the ditch when a hand grabbed her ankle and gave her a pull back into the ditch. Ellie was off-balance from the climb and fell with a hard thud into the bottom of the ditch. The wind was knocked from her lungs, and Ellie choked for air. She could feel the water from the bottom of the ditch seep into her clothes. Between the shock of the fall and the cool of the water, Ellie tried to regain her wits about her. Trying to breathe slowly through her nose and get air back into her lungs, she coughed and sputtered, trying to get her wind back.

Ellie opened her eyes to see Steve, kneeling beside her. Seeing her eyes open, Steve threw himself upon Ellie like a wolf, attacking his prey. His hands found her throat and began to squeeze what little air Ellie had from her body. Ellie reached up and grabbed anything she could, pulling his hair with one hand and clawing at his face. His grip loosened momentarily. Gasping for air, Ellie sucked in as much oxygen as she could.

Steve had only been stunned for a moment by the hair pulling and clawing of his face. Again, he grabbed for Ellie's throat. Grabbing and squeezing with both hands, he was a man bent on destruction. He was going to kill her if he could!

Ellie was trying to scream, but the hands clamped around her throat would not let her voice make a sound. Instinctively, she pulled up a knee quickly to knee him in the stomach. Her knee bounced off his side and was misdirected. This infuriated Steve. Balling his right fist, he struck Ellie in the face. His knuckles, sliding across her right cheek and right eye. The knuckles opened a gash in her cheek. Ellie saw stars and thought she would pass out from the pain. Somehow her hand reached out and grabbed the wound in his groin. Drawing her hand tight, her nails dug into the fresh and sensitive wound.

Howling like a wounded animal, Steve recoiled from the attack. Grabbing wet moss and mud in her hand, she flung the dirt and rock at Steve. Now Ellie tried to sit up. Ellie tried to get her surroundings in order. Finding a rock in her hand that she didn't remember grabbing, she brought the rock down with force against Steve's head.

Ellie was fighting for her very life. She watched as Steve seemed to go lifeless before her very eyes and crumple to the ground beside her. Inhaling deeply for the first time to catch her breath, Ellie coughed as too much oxygen was now entering her lungs. Still sitting in the mud and dirt of the ditch, Ellie turned over and got on her hands and knees. Pulling herself to her feet, Ellie's whole body now ached. Her face was swollen and painful, and she tasted blood on her lips.

Looking around, Ellie searched for the pistol she had lost during their battle. Finding it lying on the bank of the ditch, she grabbed it and wiped off some of the dirt, ejecting a shell from the gun, making sure everything still worked. She scanned the house in front of her. Not seeing anyone, she began to wonder why Howard had not come from the house when shots were fired. He could have easily helped Steve overtake her in the ditch.

Ellie now reconsidered going into the ranch house, deciding something did not feel right.

Ellie began to crawl up the ditch opposite from the house. She was going to head back to the truck and get her and her friends out of there. Her face was now bleeding pretty well. Chuck was injured. Melissa had been through hell being trapped in that secret room of a prison. Looking down at herself now bathed in moonlight, she could see that her own blouse was covered in fresh blood.

Limping back in the direction of her friends, Ellie began to hope they had not left without her. She didn't want to think of being left alone out on this nightmare of a property. So much hate and ill will had been done on this land that she just wanted to escape it and leave it behind.

On her way to the truck, Ellie began to think of who was behind all this evil and drug trade. It had to be someone that had connections and was seemingly untouchable. So far, this person had been able to stay out of everything. She would need to find out who was in charge.

First, she needed to take care of her friends and get them out of here. Ellie heard the sound of an engine starting. It sounded like the truck that Steve had driven. Nervously, she watched the hill and field for truck lights. Her heart began to race. She didn't know if she had another fight left in her.

The sound of the truck was leaving the ranch. The noise of the engine got farther and farther away from her. Ellie took a sigh of relief at knowing her attackers were leaving.

Now Ellie raced to the Explorer and found her friends worried and sitting in a shocked state. Opening the driver's side door, Ellie peered across their faces. Her friends all looked shell-shocked. Summoning her reserves of strength, Ellie smiled at her friends her best and brightest grin. It was then she realized her face must have looked a mess. Ellie started to laugh. The moment struck her as funny. She thought, *I guess I would look shell-shocked, too, if I was see the door open, and a woman looking like ground hamburger was standing there in front of me.*

Climbing in the vehicle, she started the vehicle and headed toward the ranch and not away from it. Ellie heard murmurs of resistance and opposition to the direction she had chosen. Ellie simply raised her hand to silence the group. Now was not a time for discussion. They would only have a short time for action before God knows who came back to the ranch.

Ellie hit the gas and flew across the gravel road. Crossing the wooden bridge of the drainage ditch, Ellie cranked the wheel to the left, and the tires spun as she drove along the drainage ditch. Seeing her quarry in the ditch. Ellie hit the brakes. Yelling for Jim and Shelby's help, she told Sue to get out and open the back hatch door. Guiding Jim and Shelby into the ditch, Ellie grabbed Steve's legs and instructed Jim and Shelby to grab his arms.

Together, they carried the wounded and unconscious man out of the drainage ditch. Ellie led the trio to the back of the vehicle. She told them to put Steve into the back of the vehicle. Dropping his legs, Ellie left his legs, hanging out of the back of the vehicle. Ellie grabbed a role of duct tape from the back side pocket that John Sr. had kept stocked with needed goodies, saying a private thank-you to her husband. She taped Steve's legs together and pushed his limp legs into the back of the vehicle. Throwing the tape to Jim, she instructed him to tape Steve's wrists and to make sure they were tight.

Having Steve loaded into the back of the truck. Sue closed the back door on their new captive. Telling them to load up and that they needed to get moving quickly, no one questioned Ellie. At this point, they did as they were told.

Ellie put the SUV in drive and floored it. Ellie had hit a good speed going past the ranch house. Reaching the gravel driveway that led to the Recreation Road between Wolf Creek and Craig, Ellie saw that she was doing fifty miles per hour on a gravel road. Somehow she was not nervous and had now gained a calm composure. Everyone else in the vehicle may be white knuckling the ride, but Ellie now had a sense of purpose.

Coming to a sliding turn onto the pavement of the frontage road. Ellie almost lost control of the vehicle. Screams of fright came from her friends, and Ellie took her foot off the gas.

A little.

Ellie held her vision to the road, not answering any questions. The passengers of her car got quiet. Ellie saw the silver of the Missouri River Bridge up ahead. Ellie thought she better slow the vehicle down to make the left hand corner onto to Beartooth Road that led up to Holter Lake. She was heading back to the safety of the cabin. There, she would formulate a plan and get her friends cleaned up and get them needed medical attention.

Coming to the hill that brought vehicle traffic up and over to the lake, Ellie slowed the vehicle down to the posted thirty-five miles per hour speed limit. She did this as to not gain any attention from campers and residents along the lake. Again, they would need the privacy and safety of the old hunting cabin. For now, it would give them the sanctuary and rest they so desperately needed.

Coming to the driveway of the cabin, Ellie slowed down and rolled into the driveway as if nothing had happened at all. Ellie looked back at Shelby and asked her to get the garage door opened. Shelby quickly jumped out the back door and ran up to the garage door and opened it fast. Ellie slid the vehicle into the garage and brought it to a stop in the stall. Shelby quickly closed the door behind them.

They had made it safely to the cabin with little fuss or muss. Ellie got out of the SUV and had everyone come into the cabin. Jim and Shelby carried Chuck into the living room and set him down gently onto the sofa. Together, they made Chuck as comfortable as they could.

Ellie made her way back to the garage to check on their captive.

Putting her fingers to the artery in his neck, Ellie checked for his pulse. Finding a strong pulse and easy breath coming from his chest, Ellie shut the door and returned to the house. Steve was going to be very sore, but he was fine for now.

Ellie returned to the cabin and plopped down in a kitchen chair. Seeing her friends staring at her from the living room, Ellie asked Sue, Shelby, and Jim to join her at the table. Jim sat down at the table with his daughter still in his arms and fast asleep.

PART TWO

CHAPTER TWELVE

Ellie began to lay out her plan.

She asked Jim if there was any one he trusted with his life to meet Sue and Chuck at the hospital. They needed to get him to the hospital. Jim took the cell phone from the table and began to make some calls. Listening to his phone call, the women remained silent till Jim got off the phone.

"It's all set up. My old partner, Robert, will meet you at Benefis Hospital in Great Falls. I think it's better they head to Great Falls where no one will be expecting them. Robert is going to take care of the police on that end. They will be safe in his care. He worked with me in Helena when he just got out of the police academy," explained Jim.

"Do you trust him?" Ellie asked.

"Yes. He is a good man and honest," replied Jim frankly.

"Good. Let's get Chuck into Sue's car and get him headed to the hospital."

Together, all four of them got Chuck into Sue's car. It was rough going and getting him into the back seat was not easy. Chuck let out an occasional yelp of pain, but he took it like a trooper even joking with them about it.

"I am in pain, but there is not much else you can break on me!" Chuck smiled, bringing a nervous laugh from the group.

Sue and Shelby propped pillows under Chuck's head and got him covered with a warm blanket. Sue came around the car to Ellie and pulled her into a very tight hug. It was Ellie's turn to let out a yelp of pain.

"You're hurt too! Ellie, you need to come with us and get checked along with Jim." Sue was trying to appeal to Ellie's common sense.

"I am fine. Just sore," Ellie told her best friend.

"I know you're lying to me, but I know that tone. Ellie, please be careful," said Sue.

"I will. Now get going and get that husband of yours taken care of," Ellie replied in her strongest voice, hoping the pain didn't come through.

Ellie reached out to Sue, and the two friends hugged as tears of friendship fell from their eyes. Ellie was watching as Sue got the car headed back out and to the hospital. No one moved until they could no longer see the headlights.

It was then they moved back into the cabin.

Getting back into the kitchen, they all turned as they heard yelling, coming from the garage.

"I guess our guest has awaken," Ellie spoke flatly.

Out to the garage they went to see what they unwanted guest needed.

Together, they carried Steve to the sofa where Chuck had just laid. Looking down at the sofa, Ellie pinched up her face at seeing the blood from Chuck that had soaked the cushions. She hoped and prayed that Chuck would be fine. He was strong, and she again said a silent prayer for his safety.

Steve began to protest and threaten loudly.

Having enough of this man, Ellie said, "You can sit there quietly and be our guest, or would you like another visit from the rock I used on you earlier?" Ellie meant it too. She had had enough of this evil man.

Cursing under his breath, Steve quieted down.

"That's a good gentleman, and I am using that term loosely." Ellie turned and headed back to the table for a seat in a chair.

Picking up the cell phone, Ellie looked over at her list of numbers on the wall. Finding the one she needed, she dialed the phone. Getting the answering machine, she redialed. A groggy and sleepy voice answered the phone.

"This better be good. Do you know what time it is? The voice answered the phone and not sounding happy about it."

"Hey, Dave. It's Ellie Moore, and I am up at our fishing cabin. Yes. Yes. I know it's late. I wouldn't have called if it wasn't important," Ellie replied into the phone.

"What can I do for you, Ellie?" Dave, sounding now more awake and alert.

"I have had a little accident and was wondering if you could bring your EMT bag up here and give us a once over?" Ellie asked.

"Are you hurt bad, and how many were there?" Dave asked.

"There are three of us who need some attending. I need you to come by yourself in your own vehicle and don't tell anyone where you're going, or what you're doing. I will explain later after you arrive. Dave, I really do need your help and assistance." Ellie words sounding urgent.

Ellie hung up the phone, wondering how she was going to explain this one to Dave. He would want her to go the hospital. She would cross that bridge later. For now, she needed her and Jim looked over. Plus the son of gun on the sofa needed attending. Looking over at Steve, anger rose within her. Ellie had to turn away from him. Her ire was rising, and she was determined not to let the man know he was getting the best of her. She would not sink to that man's level.

Jim was washing away some of the dried blood in the kitchen sink when Dave arrived at the cabin. Ellie could see Dave, looking around the cabin and wondering what the heck he had gotten himself into. Seeing their prisoner they had tied on the sofa, she saw that Dave was about to ask what was going on.

"Dave, I will explain, but first I need you to check out Jim and Melissa. I think Melissa is okay physically anyway," Ellie had cut him off before he could ask his question.

Seeing the police uniform that Jim was wearing, Dave headed over to attend to Jim and see to his cuts and bruises. Shelby and Ellie sat at the table as Jim was attended to by Dave. Dave let them know that Jim was okay but should get himself checked at the hospital for any internal injuries. He reminded everyone that he was just an EMT and not a doctor. He could only do some triage on them and that was all.

Coming over to Ellie, he looked upon the cut on her face. He began to clean the rock and gravel from the cut and put a temporary butterfly bandage over the cut to hold it together so it could begin to heal. He started to tell Ellie that she needed to go to the hospital. Ellie cut him off.

"No need for that. It's all just surface scratches," Ellie interjected.

Dave could see that he was going to get nowhere with Ellie, so he stopped before he started. Looking over at the man on the sofa, Dave looked at Ellie and asked what she wanted him to do with him. Ellie told Dave to get Steve cleaned up the best he could and clean and wrap his wounds. She made sure to instruct him not to remove his binds and to be careful around him.

Dave moved over to the sofa. Grabbing a scissor from his medical bag, Dave began to cut away the bloodied jeans that Steve was wearing. He started to peel away the crusty bloody jeans. The jeans had started to dry and stick to the wounds. Steve made noises of protest, and Dave went about his job. Steve realized Dave was there to help him and let him go about his job without much protest.

Dave got the wound in his groin cover. "A couple inches closer, and you might have lost one of your boys down there," pointing to Steve's crotch.

Steve simply gave Dave a quick angry smile, letting Dave know that he didn't find his comment very funny and wasn't interested. Dave just shrugged his shoulders and continued to work on the wounds.

Dave moved onto the shattered knee of Steve. Steve cried out in pain as Dave did the best he could to remove any dirt and moss from the wound. He wrapped the knee tightly. It crossed Dave's mind that this man would never use that knee properly again. It was not a pretty wound, and he knew it was bad. Using his limited medical training, he wrapped to the best of his ability.

Looking over the head wound, he cut away some of the dry and matted hair from the cut. Using a tweezer from his bag, he tried to gently remove a bit of rock fragment from the cut. Wiping away the blood and dirt, Dave broke open a small tube of antiseptic and poured the bottles contents over the gash. Steve let out a groan from the sting of the antiseptic. Wrapping a gauze bandage around his head to cover the wound, he finished his work quickly. Something about the man didn't settle well with Dave, and he wanted to be finished as quickly as possible.

Dave summoned Ellie and Jim outside. Shelby stood by the door, listening to the conversation.

"Not sure what is going on here. That man in there needs to get to a hospital. That knee is going to need surgery, and I think there is a bullet still in his upper thigh. I can't say for sure, but infection is going to start setting in on him," Dave spoke with a matter-of-fact tone.

"There is one more favor I have to ask of you, Dave," Ellie said.

"Okay," he answered.

"I need you to take Melissa with you and not let anyone know that you and Michelle have her. No one will expect her to be with you. She will be safe in your care," Ellie urgently spoke.

"What is going on, Ellie? Never mind. I don't think I want to know," Dave finished. Thinking better of it that he should not have asked the question.

Jim moved into the house and got Melissa up from the chair that she had fallen asleep in. Ellie could see Jim, talking to his little girl about what was happening. Melissa started crying and protesting. Jim let her know that he didn't want her to go either, but she would be safe with Dave and Michelle. Picking up his daughter, Jim carried Melissa out to Dave's car. Putting her in the front seat and fastening her safety belt, Jim bent over into the car and kissed his daughter on the cheek. Ellie heard Jim say, "I love you." And Melissa give a tearful reply.

The little girl had been through so much, and it was painful to watch Jim, having to send her off with a complete stranger. Melissa could be heard, yelling, "Daddy!" from the car. It was not easy to see the pain in Jim's eyes as he returned to the cabin without looking back. Ellie tried to give a word of encouragement to him. Jim just raised his hand in a move to silence her. Ellie was quiet and let Jim get his moment of silent introspection. She didn't want to pretend to understand his pain or his fear.

Jim walked into the living room of the cabin and fell into the recliner in the corner. His eyes didn't leave Steve. There was an anger, simmering inside Jim. Ellie could see the anger directed at the man who had held his daughter captive. For many minutes, Jim held a murderous look at Steve. Steve saw the look he was getting from Jim and knew better than to speak up with some stupid comment.

Ellie breathed a sigh of relief. She knew her and Shelby would not be able to stop Jim if he wanted to hurt, or kill the man, lying on her sofa. Ellie didn't think she would be able to handle the violence. It was a relief when Jim finally rose from the chair and moved to the kitchen table. Taking up a chair with his back to Steve, he rested his head in his hands and began to shake. Shelby and Ellie both gathered at his side and held him his shoulders. Ellie wanted so much to reach down and hold him like her own child. She held back because she didn't know if she herself would lose it as well. She stood and tried to remain strong for the both of them.

Looking over at Shelby, Ellie placed her hand on Shelby's shoulder and gave a squeeze of encouragement. At that, Shelby moved to the table as well and sat and began to weep. The evening was taking its toll on the three of them. So much had happened, and everyone's minds were beginning to finally process everything that had taken place.

Going around the table to Shelby, she led Shelby by the hand to one of the bedrooms off the living room. It was obvious that the girl needed some rest. Ellie got Shelby tucked into bed. Before leaving her to rest, Ellie bent over and kissed the girl on the forehead. Running her hand over her cheek, she smiled down at the girl that could be like her own daughter. Ellie began to reflect on so much they had been through together in such a short time. Ellie found herself, caring very much for the young girl. Shelby had so much spirit and goodness that it was easy to love and care about her. Ellie moved to the doorway of the bedroom. Looking back at the already sleeping girl, Ellie smiled as she turned out the light.

Ellie found herself happy that once again, they had found some relative safety. Going back out to the kitchen, she found Jim asleep at the table. Gently giving him a shake, Jim awoke with a start to find Ellie by his side. Getting Jim to the other guest bedroom was difficult. He began to protest that someone needed to watch Steve and remain alert. Ellie did her best to assure Jim that she would take care of it. Jim lay down on the bed and didn't even get under the covers. Ellie grabbed an afghan from the linen closet and covered him up.

Turning off the bedroom light, Ellie looked back at the young man, sleeping on the bed. She felt like a mother, tucking in her children for the night. Seeing that Shelby and Jim were resting and taken care of for the night, she moved to the living room to check on Steve.

Finding Steve snoring softly on the couch. Ellie surmised that he wouldn't be moving anywhere for the night. Moving to the side table, Ellie switched off the light. Walking into the kitchen, she turned off the kitchen light as well.

Making her way to her bedroom, Ellie was asleep before her head hit the pillow. Her exhaustion proved to be too much.

Adrenaline had taken its toll on all of them. They were now crashing after the adrenaline rush of the evening's adventures. Their bodies worn out and needing sleep. Their bodies knew that rest was the only way to heal the wounds. It was a well-needed rest after being inflicted with pain and a near-death experience.

It was a night of rest that they would all need.

CHAPTER THIRTEEN

Ellie awoke early just as the sun was coming up. Her phone had been ringing, and it brought her out of her peaceful slumber. Wishing it would stop, it continued to ring. Ellie moved slowly from the bed. Her bones and muscles all protesting the pain and ache they were now experiencing. She knew she was going to be sore this morning, but this was more than a couple ibuprofen would cure.

Not remembering to look at the caller ID, Ellie answered the phone. As she said hello, it dawned on her that she had been foolish in not checking the caller ID. Mentally kicking herself, she waited for the caller to say something.

"Ellie? This is Bill Wallace," his voice said from the ear piece.

"Bill? It's very early. What can I do for you?" Ellie said in response.

"I have heard you have Shelby," Bill said.

"Wait. What? How do you know that I have Shelby with me?" Surprise in her voice.

"I need to see my daughter. She and I need to have a talk about some important matters." His voice cold.

"Bill, Shouldn't your first question be, 'How is my daughter?' And second, you never answered my question about how you knew Shelby was with me." Ellie was confused in his answers.

"Ellie, you did your job. Now I want my daughter brought home immediately." Again, coldness in his voice.

"I am afraid your daughter isn't going anywhere until you tell what is going on?" Ellie said sternly.

"Listen here. I hired you to do a job. You did it. Now get my daughter back to this house immediately. Next time, I am not going to ask so nicely." Anger filling the phone. His patience lost.

"It's you. You're the boss behind Howard and Steve! It is the only way you could have known she was with me." Ellie didn't want to believe her own words.

"You have no idea what I am capable of—"

Cutting him off, she said, "I don't care what you're capable of. You would have your own daughter killed over drugs. You're her father, Bill."

"She is not my daughter. I am her stepfather. Do you think I really care what happens to that little slut? She has been a pain in my ass since she was a kid." Hate spewed from his mouth.

"What is it that you want, Mr. Wallace?" Ellie questioned. Confusion and surprise were filling her thoughts.

"I want my darling daughter brought to our home." The snide comment flowed easy from him and was not lost on Ellie.

"I am afraid that is not going to happen. You think I would place that sweet girl in your hands? The hands of a monster!" Ellie slammed the phone shut.

Ending the call, Ellie felt the shock move through her.

Turning around, Ellie saw that Shelby had been listening from the doorway of the guest room. Shelby fled to the safety of the bedroom and threw herself on the bed. Following Shelby into the bedroom, Ellie sat down next to Shelby.

The girl sobbed and cried over who she had thought had been a loving father. Who could blame the poor girl? All along, he had hated her, and now, he was willing to kill her. Ellie could only begin to imagine what the girl must now be going through. It was a terrible and painful realization for any child to have to endure. The way Bill spoke on the phone was cruel and lacked any feeling whatsoever. He spoke as if Shelby were a possession and not his child. Ellie let the girl cry out her emotions. She didn't know what she could say in such a situation. She would just sit and try to comfort her as much as possible.

Ellie's thoughts wondered back to the day Bill Wallace had come into her office. He played the caring and worried father. Ellie had taken the bait and the case. Her heart had gone out to the man that had come into her office. Now realizing that it had all been a lie,

Ellie was furious. She had been deceived and tricked into believing the man had cared for Shelby. He hadn't cared at all. He had simply been wanting to find the problem that had been affecting his cushy little drug trade. He hadn't been looking for a lost daughter. He had been looking for a lost problem that he wanted to take care of and not in a good way either.

Ellie got up from the bed and placed a blanket over Shelby. She would need some time alone to digest what had just taken place. The girl was having to deal with a whole life that was now a lie. Leaving her alone in the room, Ellie closed the door and headed to the kitchen.

Putting on a fresh pot of coffee, Ellie realized that in the ensuing phone call that she had forgotten all about her sore muscles. Now being painfully reminded, she headed to the bathroom to see if there were any aspirin or ibuprofen in the medicine cabinet. Finding some old ibuprofen, Ellie swallowed four without water, hoping they had not lost their effectiveness and would still work on her sore muscles.

Waiting for the coffee to brew, Ellie sat at the kitchen table and tried to think of how they were going to get out of this situation. As of now, they had no solid evidence to connect Bill Wallace to Howard and Steve. Sure, they could go with Jim to the police and share their stories and get Howard and Steve put away for life, but how were they going to get Bill? Ellie would need to question Shelby. But first, she needed some of that fresh coffee.

"Good morning," Jim said from behind her.

Startled from her thoughts, Ellie said, "Uh, good morning."

"Penny for your thoughts?" Jim replied.

"It's been an interesting morning. Let's get you a cup of coffee, and we will talk," Ellie said as she reached into the cupboard for a mug for Jim.

Jim's eyebrows were raised in a questioning look as he said, "Okay."

Sitting down at the table with the coffee, Ellie shared with Jim about the conversation she had just had with Shelby's stepfather. Jim listened while sipping his coffee. He didn't ask any question and waited for Shelby to finish.

"Now it's starting to make sense," Jim said with his chin, resting in his hand.

"What is making sense?" Ellie asked.

"Well, we have been wondering where the leak was coming from on the drug task force. Bill Wallace is on the board for the task force. All operations have to be run through the board first before being given the go head to be put into operation out in the field. Given his position, he would know exactly when and where operations were being put into place. He would also have access to our informant lists."

Ellie sat back amazed at what Jim was telling her. She had no idea.

Jim continued.

"Bill must have been checking the informant lists and watching to see if anyone was getting close to his operation. That's how he let Steve and Howard know of our guy on the inside. It never even dawned on me to think of him. He had always come across as a family man and someone who was ardently opposed to drugs. Here he is. The Montana kingpin. I would have never guessed that in a million years."

Ellie looked over to see Steve, listening intently to their conversation. Moving over to the sofa, Ellie ripped the duct tape away from his mouth.

"You knew this all the time and didn't even think to look out for Shelby!" Ellie was now yelling at Steve.

"What was I supposed to do? Her dad wanted me to keep an eye on her," Steve answered.

"You're a piece of filth!" Spit flying from Ellie's mouth.

Jim stepped in and replaced the tape back over Steve's mouth. Placing his hands on Ellie's shoulders, Jim led Ellie back to the kitchen table.

CHAPTER FOURTEEN

Bill Wallace was still simmering from his phone call with Ellie. Howard had let him know that Shelby was now in the company of his private detective. He had wanted to remain calm on the phone and was pissed off that he had given away his hand on the first sentence.

Stomping out of the house, Bill stormed out of the house. Hitting the screen door to the porch with full speed, he nailed it with his fist and the momentum of his body. The door flew open, smacking the wall with a clap of board against board. His strength broke the wood door from the hinges. *The ole wife isn't going to be happy with that one*, he thought.

Standing on the porch, he surveyed his damage to the door. He needed to calm down and think straight before getting in his pick-up truck. The muscles in his shoulders and neck tensed whenever he thought of Shelby. He never liked the girl. *Parading around in those skimpy little swimsuits!* His mind was racing.

Bill thought back to the day when his wife had gone off to the store, and he had been watching Shelby sunbathe out in the yard. "Sure, I had had a few too many beers," he told himself.

Bill started to mutter, "That slut sat out there in the yard just flaunting herself in front of me. I am a grown man, and I have urges, just like any other red-blooded American male. Laying out there, just inviting me to come out and play with her."

His blood pressure, climbing as he thought back.

He had walked out in the yard and started talking to Shelby. She had been teasing him, he thought. *When he got out there, the little bitch had the nerve to try and cover herself with a towel. He had only been sliding his had up her thigh. What was the harm in that? She didn't need to get all pissed off and threaten to tell her mother if he ever touched her again.*

Snapping out of his thoughts, Bill turned around and walked at a fast clip to his truck. Sliding into the driver's seat, he started the vehicle and threw it into drive. Gravel flying from the tires, the tail of the truck slid around in a donut. Now facing the road, Bill slammed on the gas. Hitting the pavement, the truck tires squealed and lurched to find a grip. The back end doing a little fish tail before straightening out, the engine could be heard roaring under the hood.

The boss would be pissed when finding out that he had screwed up in getting Shelby back home. It was an unpleasant thought that he didn't want to think about right now.

For now, he would head out to Howard's and deal with that problem.

He would have to deal with the other issue later.

This wasn't supposed to be how his life was supposed to turn out. The drug running came along at a time that Bill really needed the money. He was behind on the mortgage and the real estate taxes. Every day he was getting letters from the bank, threatening that repossession of their home was soon at hand. The tax collector was threatening a sheriff's sale of the property. He would be damned if he was going to lose the house.

Fate had intervened that day when the boss had come to him and talked about some plans to make a lot of money. Seemed easy enough then. But now looking back, Bill wasn't so sure. He didn't mind people, having to die to protect himself. He just didn't like to do it himself. That's where Howard and Steve had come in handy.

Howard was psychotic and loved to be able to torture people. Bill had never met someone who got off on torturing and causing pain to other people. Truth be told, Howard gave Bill the creeps. He looked at Howard as an insurance policy and a necessary evil in his life. The boss didn't even know that Howard was on Bill's payroll. If the Boss knew, Bill would have one hell of a time, explaining his role in all this.

Steve did anything for the right amount of cash laid in front of him. Seemed the only thing the boy really cared about. Bill thought,

That Steve would screw over his mama to get to a dollar bill. As long as the money was steady, Bill knew that he didn't have to worry about Steve.

Sooner or later, those were two loose ends that he would have to tie up. He would dispose of them when it was time. For now, they were still serving a purpose. Bill liked not having to get his hands too dirty, and he got to take credit for their work. It was a win-win situation for him.

Bill thought about where Steve might be and hoped he wasn't singing like a songbird. If he was, it was the last song he would sing. *Ever!*

Bill thought he better get a hold of the cleaner. He hoped he was still in the country. It was going to cost him a pretty penny to take care of the problem. *It was worth it!* He thought to get rid of Shelby, Howard, and Steve. He wasn't going to forget about that damn Ellie Moore either. She would be a problem that he would enjoy taking care of himself.

CHAPTER FIFTEEN

Ellie was more angry now than she had been in a long time. How could a father give up his daughter for a few dollars? The thought was inconceivable to her. Plus this man tied up on her sofa, how could he be so heartless? She knew she was dealing with men who had lost their souls long ago. It was the only answer she could find for the evil things these three men were capable of.

Ellie went to look in on Shelby and see how she was doing after the shocking news she had heard. As Ellie peered in the door, she saw that Shelby was still lying in the fetal position on the bed. Moving softly across the bedroom toward the bed, Ellie was trying not to startle the stressed girl on the bed.

Sitting down on the edge of the bed, Ellie gave Shelby a light shake to awaken her. Shelby's eyes opened wide. Like that of a tiger being caught in a trap, Ellie tried to sooth her with some calming words. It took several moments for Shelby to realize where she was and that she was safe. A realization came back into her eyes as Shelby looked up at Ellie. Seeing Ellie sitting next to her on the bed, she sat up and pulled Ellie into a hug.

Both knew this was a stressful time and that now they would need to depend on each other more than ever. If they were going to come out of this alive, it was each other that they would have to depend on for their very lives!

Getting up from the bed, Ellie told Shelby to rest for a bit longer, but they may be heading out in a little bit. Shelby gave Ellie a questioning expression but didn't ask where they may be going. Instead, Shelby laid her head back down on the pillow. Shelby couldn't and didn't want to think of where they may be going. It was much easier for her to lie back on the bed and go off into the darkness of sleep.

Ellie came out of Shelby's bedroom. Just as Jim was getting off the phone, Jim asked Ellie to join him out on the front deck, overlooking the lake. Out of earshot of Steve, Jim began to tell Ellie what his immediate plan was for him and Steve. Jim would be having another deputy he trusted pick him up. They would be taking Steve to the hospital where he would remain under armed guard. He pointed out that she and Shelby would again be on their own for the time being.

Jim told Ellie that he needed to get back to Helena and find out what was happening. He also needed to update the sheriff on the events of the evening. He also wanted to work out something for Shelby and Ellie so they would be protected.

*****

Ellie watched Jim and the other deputy load Steve into the back of the police car. Standing and watching from just inside the doorway, Ellie made sure that no one could see her from the street. Ellie stood there, having the feeling of a fugitive. She reminded herself that she was one of the good guys and sometimes one had to be extra careful. It was beginning to be hard to know who to trust.

Waving to Jim in the passenger seat of the police car, she watched as they backed out of the driveway and onto Beartooth Road. Ellie got that sinking feeling in her stomach that she and Shelby were going to need to get away from the cabin. Too many people knew they were there. It was becoming a liability for them to stay there much longer.

Back in the cabin, Ellie reached under the cabinet and grabbed the first bag she found. In the bag, she stuffed as much food and drink as it would carry. Her sixth sense was telling her to move. So far, that little voice inside her had been right. She figured that now was no time to stop listening.

Calling to Shelby, Ellie grabbed her go bag off the table and checked the contents again, zipping the zipper up tight and setting it next to the bag of food. Turning around to get Shelby up out of bed, she found Shelby, standing next to the table. Busy in her work, Ellie didn't even hear Shelby walk across the creaky floor of the cabin. Ellie made a mental check to not let that happen again. Now was no time to not be paying attention.

She told Shelby to grab a few blankets and pillows and put them in the back seat of the SUV. Shelby was hearing the nervous tension in Ellie's voice. Moving quickly, Shelby knew that Ellie was moving fast for a reason. Shelby wasn't going to wait around and ask questions. Something was happening. She knew enough to move quickly.

Fifteen minutes later, the women had the SUV loaded and were on the road. Ellie happened to glance down at the gas gauge and realized they were going to need gas if they wanted to get anywhere. Ellie was nervous of stopping done at the Wolf Creek Gas Station but knew it was the only service station around for miles. They would have to chance it. The whole idea of having to stop in Wolf Creek made her nervous. They would be too exposed and out in the open for anyone to see. Whoever drove by could easily see who was at the gas station.

Pulling up to the inside gas stall closest to the entrance of the gas station, Ellie quickly pulled her credit card from her wallet. Sliding the credit card into the pump, Ellie's eyes continued to scan the surrounding parking lot. Letting the pump run until gas shot out of the overflow by the gas cap, she knew it was now as full as it was going to get. Twisting the gas cap back into place, Ellie closed the gas cap door and hurried back into the front seat of the pickup. She was not going to fart around while there were people out there who wanted them dead.

Ellie began pulling the vehicle away from the gas pump when Shelby let out a gasp.

"There's my dad! I mean Bill." She was looking over at Ellie with the look of help and fear in her eyes.

"Push your seat back. Quickly! There is a lever on the side that you just pull up and it—"

"Got it!" Shelby cut in as the seat back dropped toward the seat behind her.

Ellie pulled the truck out onto Recreation Road in front of the gas station. Trying to act like there was no problem, Ellie had to control her foot with all her might. Her foot was trying to override her brain by wanting to step hard on the gas pedal. Ellie watched her mirrors intently to see if the truck Bill Wallace was in would follow them.

Ellie was just passing by the local bar when she checked her mirrors one last time. Glancing in the mirror, she saw the large truck scream out onto the road in their direction. This time, her foot and her brain didn't have to communicate. Her foot was already on the gas before her brain had a chance to say anything.

The back end of the SUV came around as Ellie was going too fast for the corner by the fire hall just pass the bar. She had been trying to get around the corner as it led to the on-ramp of the freeway. Interstate 15 was only seventy-five yards away, and now, she was facing the predator who had gotten wind of them. Seeing the large truck coming fast right at them, Ellie again stepped on the gas. Aiming her vehicle right for the truck Bill was driving straight at them. It was going to be a close game of chicken! Ellie knew the stakes of this deadly game and kept her eyes on the man in the truck ahead of her. Shelby could see Ellie, driving with an intent look on her face. She grabbed the oh-shit handle with white knuckles. Her other hand was clutching the center column between her and Ellie. Fear racing through Shelby as she was only a spectator to this game. Her knees were involuntarily pulling up from the seat toward her chests.

It seemed the trucks were destined to crash into one another in a groaning crash of twisted metal. At the last moment, Ellie pulled the wheel to the right and just narrowly escaped the front of Bill's truck by mere inches. The back wheels grabbed gravel as she righted the vehicle back on to the paved road. Ellie looked in the mirror just in time to see the truck Bill was driving hit the telephone pole on the corner. Watching as the truck was slammed to a halt and the back wheels, coming up off the ground, Ellie let out a whoop of delight!

This round of chicken had gone to Ellie.

Bill sat in the truck stunned after hitting the pole. He had been so intent on hitting the other truck that he didn't even see the pole until the last moment. His foot had just gotten to the brakes as the nose of the truck began to crinkle like tissue paper against the wood of the pole. The next thing he saw was the airbag in his face as his body was still moving through the air. Stunned by the accident, Bill sat silently in the truck.

Pushing the door open with his legs, Bill grabbed the cell phone off the seat. Standing now in the parking lot of the Wolf Creek Fire Hall, Bill quickly dialed the phone.

"How fast can you be in Montana?" he said into the phone.

"I am on my way!" the cleaner said back into the phone.

"Good. I have got two little bitches that need cleaning up after!"

Slamming the phone shut, Bill walked over to the bar for a drink. He now felt a little better that a professional was going to be handling his problem.

CHAPTER SIXTEEN

Ellie picked up her cell phone and dialed the number fast. Talking quickly into the phone, she made plans for her and Shelby to hide out until they could come up with a better plan.

It had been Sue on the phone.

Ellie told Shelby her plan. They were heading to Sue and Chuck's hunting cabin out back in the Dearborn River area. Ellie really didn't have much of a plan. She was still trying to figure out who they could trust. Until she spoke with Jim again, it was hard to know who to trust. Questions kept circling like vultures in Ellie's mind.

Getting to the Dearborn exit off Interstate 15, Ellie had been watching her mirrors for a tail. Thankfully, there had been little traffic on the freeway. It made watching the cars much easier. She felt safe that they hadn't been followed. She was sure that Bill was working on something. But what? For now, they would get a bit of a reprieve from the action.

Reaching Sue and Chuck's place on the river, Ellie thought how nice of a place it would be if they weren't running for their lives. It was a typical two-story log cabin situated right on the river. After getting settled in, both women moved to the covered front porch, facing the river. Together, they enjoyed the silence of their surroundings and took in the flowing river.

Shelby broke the silence.

"Do you have a plan?"

"Not yet. I'm trying to put everything in perspective. A lot has happened, and I need to wrap my mind around it. I keep feeling like we are missing a piece of the puzzle. Maybe it's just the stress of the last couple days. Either way, my gut is telling me that trouble will soon be heading our way!"

Ellie turned back from Shelby and drifted back into thought and took in the peaceful surroundings of the cabin and the river.

CHAPTER SEVENTEEN

Steve had come, too, in the hospital. At first, he was unaware of his surroundings. He found his belly itched and went to move his right hand to relieve the itch. Finding his hand handcuffed to the bed rail, he let out a sigh and said, "Shit!" under his breath. This may be a harder situation for him to get out then he first imagined.

Using the remote for the adjustable bed, he brought the head of the bed up into the sitting position. Steve's eyes began to swim from the pain and the drugs that were flowing through his IV. Breathing in through his nose and exhaling through his mouth, he fought the pain. Even with the pain he was now feeling, it still felt better to be off his ribs and in the sitting position. Adjusting the pillows behind with his one free arm, he thought he would watch some TV since he wasn't going anywhere soon.

His stomach began to rumble. Pushing the call button that was attached to the bed, he waited for the nurse to come to his room. Seeing that nothing of real interest was on the television, Steve began to grow anxious and was wondering what was keeping the nurse.

Looking up from the television to see his room door, Steve was about to say, "What took you so long?" when he realized that his visitor was not the one he wanted. Instead of the nurse, he looked up to see the sheriff's deputies enter his room.

Entering the room, Jim looked at the bed and gave Steve a smile. He was happy to see the boy had survived to rat out his bosses. Along with Jim came his old partner, Pat Hendricks. Jim and Pat had started together at the sheriff's department right around the same time. Over the years, they had pulled each other out of some tight spots, saving each other's lives more than once. Jim trusted Pat with his life and was glad to have Pat along for this interview.

"Steve, looks like you're feeling better?" Jim spoke to Steve.

"Either of you got a cigarette?" Steve asked, looking annoyed.

"Sorry, but I just don't think that would be a good idea. Might want to let the lungs heal before you start to wreck them," Jim said flatly.

Pat jumped in. "Steve, we are here to make a deal with you. It's no bull and is signed by the DA's office."

"I don't have a thing to say," said Steve, staring anywhere but at the officers.

Jim broke in, "Right now, you're facing kidnapping, second degree murder of our informant, assaulting an officer, and quite a few more. Do you want me to go on?"

Steve looked up at Jim. Fear was starting to sink into the boy. Jim could see the twinge of fear float across his eyes. Jim tried not to smile at Steve's predicament.

"This offer isn't going to last long. I can tell you that. I wouldn't wait too long to talk. The DA is willing to reduce your charges and sentence. *If* you decide to cooperate," Jim said.

"I would be a snitch, and I would be as good as dead in prison. All that deal is doing is signing my death sentence. If I don't get killed before the trial, I would be killed in prison. Talk to me when you have something better to offer. Now get out!" Steve spoke with the voice of a man who knew he was doomed.

"Either way, looks like you put yourself in a pickle this time. You think if we get Howard first that he is going to wait around for a better deal? He is going to sell you out in a minute! Think about it," Jim said as he turned for the door.

Out in the hall, Jim told Pat that they would let him stew in his own juices for a little bit. They would check on him later when Steve had had a little time to think about his situation.

Back in the hospital room, Steve lie in bed, thinking over the offer. Either way, he was dead, but at least, he would get to prison alive. Or so he hoped.

Watching TV for a couple hours. Steve drifted back off to sleep. The pain medicine was catching up to him. Not wanting to think about his situation any longer, he gave into sleep. His eyes had grown too heavy to keep open any longer.

*****

Coming up the back stairs of the hospital was the cleaner. Dressed in a doctor's white coat, he looked as if he fit right in with the hospital staff. He was still careful not to be seen. It was always better to have little or no complications of witnesses. Trying to make his job as easy as possible, it was better to get in and out before being seen.

Over the years, the cleaner had found that it was easier not to be seen and then have to tie up any loose ends. If he couldn't do this, he also found that it was easier to hide in plain sight. To blend in and act like you belong, nobody questions you when you look as if you belong there.

A flight up the stairs, two nurses entered the stairwell and were coming down the stairs toward the cleaner. Ducking into hallway just off the stairs, he watched as the nurses passed his doorway without noticing a thing. Sliding back into the stairwell, the cleaner made his way to the third floor.

Before opening the door to the third floor, he checked the hallway while looking through the small glass window in the door. The cleaner watched for any nurses or staff in the hallway. Sitting outside the room of his target was a sheriff's deputy. This might be a bit trickier than he thought. Opening the door, the cleaner walked down the hall as if he belonged there.

Coming up to Steve's room, he spoke to the deputy, "How is our patient this afternoon?"

"Quiet," the deputy said back.

"Good to hear," the cleaner spoke confidently.

Taking Steve's chart from the wall. He opened the door to the room and entered. Seeing his target, lying in bed asleep, the cleaner moved around the bed to the IV pole. Taking an empty syringe from his pocket, he pulled back the plunger of the syringe. He slid the need into the injection point at his wrist. Depressing the plunger, air was injected into Steve's blood stream.

Awakening with a fear of death in his eyes, Steve knew it was too late. Looking up into the eyes of the man dressed as a doctor, Steve knew the man had just killed him. A sudden pain rushed through his body as the air bubbles flew to his heart.

Seeing Steve's eyes open, the cleaner placed a pillow over his victims face to muffle any scream. No scream was heard, just a small moan and tensing of the body, then the victim went limp and into the deep sleep of death. It happened all very quickly and easily, just the way the cleaner liked it. No fuss. No muss.

Removing the needle and syringe from the injection port of the IV, the cleaner put the syringe back in his pocket. Placing the pillow back under Steve's head, he made his now-dead victim to look like he was sleeping.

Moving back across the room to the door, the cleaner had almost forgot the chart. Grabbing the chart from the bed table, he placed the chart back in its holder as he left the room.

He was smiling at the officer and saying, "Good day!" He smiled again and headed toward the stairs. Shedding his procured jacket in the stairwell, the cleaner moved down the stairs and out of the hospital. It had been a clean and easy job, just the way he liked it.

*****

Jim found Steve, lying asleep in bed. He walked over to the bed and shook him. It was time to wake him up and get some answers from him. Not seeing any movement, Jim gave Steve a more vigorous shake. Noticing that Steve's shoulder felt cold, he reached for his wrist and checked for a pulse. Not finding a pulse, Jim yelled for the deputy outside the door.

The deputy entered the room and asked, "What is up?"

"What the hell do you mean, 'What is up?' This man is dead. That's what is up!" Jim was pissed off.

"What do you mean dead? The doctor was just in here checking on him," spoke the deputy.

"What doctor? When?" Jim asked.

"He left just a couple minutes ago. He headed toward the stairs."
The deputy pointed in direction of the stairwell.

Jim fled the room and raced for the stairwell. Looking over the
edge of the stairs, Jim looked up and down and watched for movement. Seeing some white on the stairs, Jim ran down the stairs, taking two and three stairs at a time. Finding the discarded jacket on the
stairs and swearing at his find, Jim flew down the rest of the stairs to
the doorway that led to back parking lot of the hospital.

Scanning the parking lot for any signs of a person, Jim swore for
the world to hear. Kicking the door with his cowboy boot, Jim knew
the perp was long gone.

"Son of a bitch!"

Only Pat and the sheriff knew about Steve's location. Jim's mind
began to race. Pat. Why did Pat have to leave suddenly after they left
the hospital? It didn't make any sense.

"Son of a bitch!" Frustration flooding his voice.

Jim couldn't believe that his partner of all these years was the
department snitch. Damn. He was the godfather to Pat's kids. Jim
knew it was not the sheriff. She was sick of the drugs in the county
and would not jeopardize her position for this. It had to be Pat.

Grabbing his cell phone from his pocket, he dialed Pat's cell
phone number. Getting his answering service, Jim nearly threw his
cell phone across the parking lot. Just before releasing the phone into
the air, Jim tighten his grip.

"Ellie and Shelby!"

Dialing Ellie's cell phone number as fast as his fingers would
dial, Jim waited for the call to connect. It connected and went right
to voice mail. This time, the cell phone wasn't so lucky. It came to its
end while meeting the back cement wall of the hospital. Jim's frustration level had reached its peak.

Even before the fragments of plastic and phone could hit the
pavement of the parking lot, Jim was headed to his car.

Chapter Eighteen

Ellie still was sitting on the deck. Again, her stomach was telling her that something was wrong. She couldn't quite place it but knew from the last couple days that now was no time to give up on her senses. Continuing to stare out over the river, Ellie knew they would have to do something. She and Shelby couldn't hide forever. They needed to get some evidence to end this situation.

Ellie was jerked from her thoughts when the sound of a car engine invaded her thoughts. Looking up at the driveway, she first made out the light bar of a police car. Sighing to herself, she knew that Jim would know what to do. Getting up to meet Jim, Ellie stood at the stairs on the edge of the deck. Ellie watched the police car pull into the drive in front of the cabin.

Realizing that it wasn't Jim, Ellie tried to not let her face portray her worry. The car came to a halt, and the front driver's door opened. Getting out of the car, Pat gave Ellie a wave. Ellie smiled and waved and said hello. Her mind was racing. She hadn't told Jim or Pat where they were going. How did Pat know she was here? Something in this situation wasn't right.

Keeping her calm, Ellie invited Pat up onto the porch for a seat. His demeanor didn't reveal anything. But something wasn't right. Ellie could feel and sense the trouble, but Ellie thought she would sit and see what he had to say. Sitting back in the chair on the deck, Ellie waited for Pat to have a seat as well. Sitting down, she watched as Pat fidgeted in his chair. It was the first glimpse Ellie saw of Pat being nervous. Instantly, her stomach did a flip. Damn!

Seeing Shelby standing in the door behind Pat, Ellie gave Shelby a quick warning glance. Shelby saw the look on Ellie's face and somewhat retreated back away from the door. Shelby stood just ought of his eyesight but kept her vigil by the door. By now, Shelby knew Ellie enough to keep quiet and out of sight. Something was happening on porch, but Shelby didn't know what.

Looking around, Pat asked where Shelby had gotten herself to. Ellie tried to give nothing away in her answer. Ellie was thinking that two can play this game.

"She was sleeping earlier. I think the stress of the situation has gotten to the poor girl. I thought I heard the back door close earlier. She may have went for a walk down by the river. Probably do her some good to get some exercise and stretch her tired muscles," Ellie answered calmly.

"The girl has been through a lot lately." A nervous tension just barely audible in Pat's voice.

"This is true," Ellie answered honestly. Seeing Pat looked off toward the river, Ellie took a moment to glance up Shelby by the door. Shelby gave Ellie a thumbs-up signal and a quick smile.

Shelby was wondering why Ellie had lied to Pat. He was a sheriff's deputy. Standing there beyond the doorway out of sight, it dawned on her that something must be up. She trusted Ellie with her life. Ellie had now saved her more than once, and she knew enough not to betray her silence. Looking out the screen door, Shelby could see the nervous look on Ellie's face every time Pat looked away. Shelby knew she needed to find Ellie's gun.

Looking around the main room of the cabin, Shelby was looking for Ellie's purse. Seeing it on the counter, Shelby made her way silently to the breakfast bar where her purse lay. Watching the open screen door to the porch, Shelby cursed silently every time a board would creak. Hoping that it would not give away her position, the creeks and groans were barely audible, but in Shelby's mind, they roared like freight train.

Pat must have heard the creek of the floor too. He sprang out of his chair. Pulling his gun, he swung the door open. Seeing Shelby standing at the counter, he still portrayed his innocence. Looking from Shelby to the purse on the counter, Pat saw the butt of the pistol, jutting out from just inside the purse.

"Shelby, you scared me. You can never be too careful." Talking to Shelby, Pat moved deftly between Shelby and the weapon.

From behind them.

"Shelby, did you enjoy your walk?" Ellie said to Shelby while really trying to get Pat's attention away from her purse. She had seen that Pat saw the gun in her bag.

"It is so beautiful out here," Shelby said.

Moving to the fridge, Shelby pretended to be thirsty and grabbed a bottled water out of the fridge. Closing the fridge, Shelby pretended to accidentally knock the purse off the counter and onto the floor. Shelby slid the pistol under the lip of the cupboard on the floor. Picking up the purse, she placed it back on the counter.

Looking at Ellie, Shelby said, "Sorry about knocking your purse over. I guess I am still a bit nervous."

"That's all right. Nothing in there to be worried about anyway," Ellie said as she moved to the sofa. Again, Ellie hoped her fear hadn't betrayed her.

Seeing Ellie move to the sofa, Pat followed her and sat in the recliner. Not saying anything, Pat sat back in the chair and relaxed and swung the side handle back to raise the foot rest. His eyes never left Ellie. She looked over at Pat and smiled. Ellie knew they were now both in a dance for their lives. Again!

"Ellie, do you know if Chuck and Sue have any more garbage bags for the trash?" Shelby questioned.

Seeing Shelby give a quick downward glance of her eyes, Ellie responded. Shelby hoped that Ellie would catch her meaning.

"Look under the sink. I think I remember seeing them by the cleaning supplies under the sink." Ellie gave her a quizzical look.

"Thanks."

Shelby bent over behind the counter. She was out of the eyesight of Pat. Pulling out her shirt that was tucked into her jeans, Shelby quickly grabbed the pistol she had stashed earlier and placed it in her waistband at the small of her back. About to stand back up, Shelby had almost forgotten to grab a garbage bag. Quickly grabbing one from the open roll, she flung the bag in the air with both hands to open up the bag. Placing it in the garbage can, she threw away her empty water bottle. She had pretended to drink it but had poured it down the sink.

Ellie sat silently watching Shelby. Ellie tried not to smile as she realized the girl was one quick cookie. She watched as Shelby then moved to the downstairs bedroom.

"Ellie. Do you know where Sue keeps the blankets?" Shelby's voice came from inside the bedroom.

"I think there in the closet. Let me take a look. I know she keeps the cabin full of extras for company," Ellie answered back.

Looking down at Pat, she said, "Would you like one as well?"

Pat had shook his head no, so Ellie walked past him in the recliner. Moving toward the bedroom, she almost screamed when Shelby nearly pulled her arm off while trying to get her in the room. Before Ellie could get her bearings, Shelby was quickly removing the pistol from her back and handing it to Ellie.

Ellie quickly took the pistol and placed it in her waistband. Reaching over to Shelby, she used her hands to let her know to tuck back in her shirt. She didn't want to give Pat any reason to think that they were on to him. After making sure Shelby's shirt was tucked back in, Ellie moved to the closet and was grabbing a couple of blankets off the shelf when Pat entered the room.

"On second thought, I would like a small blanket," Pat said coyly. He quickly scanned the room and took the blanket Ellie had handed him.

The funny thing about this whole situation was that the cabin was hot, and no one really needed a blanket. Keeping the whole game moving, Ellie handed Shelby an extra blanket and took one for herself. She then slipped past Pat who was now standing in the doorway, watching them. He seemed to be standing there, waiting for the two to make a move. Giving him no cause, Ellie and Shelby moved into the living room and again took up seats on the sofa. Pat followed and retook his position in the recliner.

Ellie was sitting on the sofa, adjusting the blanket over her legs. Already sweating in the heat, she hoped that Pat would not take notice. Ellie removed the gun from her back while pretending to adjust a pillow and quickly stashed in under the blanket. Now it was within easy reach. Now Ellie needed and wanted some answers from Pat.

Finally, she spoke.

"Pat, how did you know we were here?" Ellie asked.

A look of surprise came over Pat's face and had quickly vanished. It was the quick flash of fear in his eyes that really betrayed him.

"Jim gave me a head's up that this may be where you're heading," he said.

"How did Jim know? I never told him." Ellie gave him a quizzical look.

Getting up from his chair, Pat moved to the picture window that looked out over the river. Ellie saw that his eyes never left her reflection in the window. He looked out over the landscape before responding. His movements now steady and controlled.

Turning around to face Shelby and Ellie, Pat answered her question.

"This is not exactly how I wanted things to turn out. I was hoping that you wouldn't think it too odd about my showing up here."

Pat moved from the window to the back of the recliner. His hands squeezed the cushion on the top of the chair. His face looked troubled and full of doubt and thought.

"Some years ago," he began, "I was involved in a shooting. I started using drugs to cope with the pain of killing a man. Before I knew it, I was so in debt and had racked up a huge bill to my dealer.

"That was when I was approached by Shelby's stepdad. He came to me with a way to get rid of what I owed on my drug debt. It was simple at first. All I had to do was give him a call when I found out or heard where and when a raid was going to happen. I had wondered why he needed me when he was on the drug task force.

"It wasn't hurting anyone, and this was a way to keep my problem from my family and the guys on the force. If any of my coworkers would have found out, I would have lost my job. My wife would have found out and would have taken the kids and left me."

He continued while a single tear fell from his eye and slid down his cheek. It was a tear from a life that had gone horribly wrong. His mouth was telling the story, but his thoughts were reflecting on a life that had not worked out as planned.

"Then Jim happened to give me a call, and I got lucky. I called your dad and said I had some info that he may want. I told him that if he released me from my debt that I would help him out one last time. Then I was out for good."

"That still doesn't tell us how you found us." Ellie looked at him.

"I suppose it doesn't matter, but when we were at your cabin, I placed a GPS tracking device under your car. It was all pretty easy. Jim never expected me. Once the device was in place, it was pretty easy to track your movements without you knowing," he said with pride in his voice.

"So you're here to kill us?" Ellie said with disdain in her voice.

"Nope. I just had to make sure you stay here until the cleaner arrives. He will make sure you disappear and get rid of any evidence," Pat replied.

"The cleaner?" Shelby asked, looking at Ellie.

Pat responded first.

"He is the guy your dad calls when your dad has a problem that he can't take care of by himself. Now it seems that you two have become his new problem."

Ellie turned back to Pat and said, "All this over drugs? You're going to make us wait for a man to come and kill us? Don't you think that if you would have gone to the sheriff originally that they would have helped you! Instead, you take the easy way out. Not so easy, was it?"

"You're probably right. Who knows now," Pat said dejectedly.

"Don't you want to make things right, and help us out of this mess?" Ellie implored.

"Make things right? Things will never be right now. You don't know the man that is coming after you. I am as good as dead, too, if I help you!" Pat said while coldly staring at Ellie, but fear had betrayed the cold stare.

"You're as good as dead now. Look at yourself, Pat. You gave up your life the moment you started helping them!" Ellie was pissed.

Ellie couldn't help but feel some semblance of pity for the man in front of her. He had first destroyed his life with drugs and then again tried to destroy it by siding with drug dealers. The man was clearly on a mission of self-destruction. Ellie had hoped that she would be able to reach him. After seeing the look he gave her, Ellie realized that it was again the look of man who had given up years ago. It's hard to reason with a man who has given up on life. Ellie had to give him a glimmer of hope. A way out.

Pat was a man that had been so afraid to kill himself to get away from his problems. He was still looking for a way to kill himself without actually having to pull the trigger. Ellie knew that when someone was hell bent on destroying themselves, it came down to that individual to pull himself out of the mire that had become their life. Only Pat could save Pat. Ellie knew that they would have to get out of the way, or go down with Pat's sinking ship.

Trying one last time to reach Pat, Ellie said, "Pat, addiction is hard. After my husband died, I didn't want to live any longer. I stayed in bed, didn't eat, and wanted to die. My addiction was self-pity. I was so focused on losing my husband that I didn't get to see all the wonderful years we had together. I had to start looking at the good times and remember the love. Pat, think of your family and remember that love and understanding. It is never too late." Compassion was filling her voice.

Pat broke down. For what looked like the first time in years, the man sobbed and was getting out so much grief that had been bottled within him. Shelby and Ellie looked at each other. Shelby grasped Ellie's hand and gave her a knowing smile.

Truth be told, Shelby and Ellie both shed a few tears as well. It was an emotional moment. It was one of those times where the air in the room was snapping with electricity. The two women sat and watched firsthand the emotional breaking of man that had carried so much of his past on his shoulders. It was difficult to hear and watch.

Ellie got up from the sofa and moved over to Pat by the recliner. Placing her hand on his arm, Ellie pulled Pat up from the chair. When she got Pat to face her, she reached out and hugged the broken man. In the grip of the hug, the man began to whimper and cry more. Ellie was holding a broken man. His spirit would take years to mend and recover, if it could be mended at all. Time would tell.

Ellie looked over at Shelby who was still sitting on the couch and sharing the grief of the moment. Shelby thought of her father, or the man she had thought was her father. He had destroyed so many lives. Drugs and money had torn her life apart. Shelby could sympathize with the man now in Ellie's arms. All the love that she had thought that Bill had given her over the years had been a lie. Shelby began to think of her family life and could not discern what was real and what was fake.

An anger boiled in Shelby. How could a man do this to his family? How could he do this to other families? It was then Shelby really realized that her stepfather was a monster who deserved no sympathy. Any familial connection that she may have felt toward the man who was supposedly her father was now gone.

CHAPTER NINETEEN

S lowly making his way along the river to the cabin, the cleaner was mad as hell that he had to chase down these two women in this heat. It would be another mile before he reached the cabin, and he began to hope that the sun would begin to fade.

He would make these targets pay for having him have to endure the heat and the bugs of the riverfront. Looking down at his arms, they were now covered in bug bites.

If that wasn't enough, the cleaner had kicked up an active hornet's nest in an old log. He had had to dive into the cool water to escape the stinging creatures that wanted to cause him pain. With each sting, his anger only increased.

Rounding a bend, the cleaner finally saw the cabin of his new prey in the distance. He would be glad to kill them both and finally be able to get back to his life. He would also make sure that Bill paid handsomely for all his troubles.

CHAPTER TWENTY

Ellie moved Pat back into the recliner and headed to the kitchen to get him some water. It was while pouring some water from the faucet into the glass that she caught a glint of something along the river.

Shelby saw the look of fear come over Ellie's face. Moving quickly to the window, her eyes tried to find what had made Ellie afraid. Shelby couldn't see anything except the glare of bottle down river. It wasn't until the bullet broke the window alongside her that she realized it was the scope of a rifle.

Both women ducked to the floor, and Shelby heard Ellie yell for her to stay down. Hearing crawling on the floor, Shelby watched as Ellie crawled up alongside her. Slowly and carefully, both women looked over the sill of the broken window. Not seeing anything, Ellie whispered for Shelby to get the gun off the sofa. Ellie had left it there when she had moved over to console Pat.

Shelby crawled along the dining table and over to the couch. Grabbing the gun off the sofa, Shelby saw that Pat was still sitting in the reclining chair, and he was still crying and distraught. The man was so out of it. Shelby realized that he hadn't even known that a bullet had just shattered the window and lodged itself in the far back wall of the cabin. Placing her hand on his knee, Shelby shook his leg vigorously to get his attention. Seeing that the man was not even realizing he was being shaken, Shelby stood on her knees and grabbed his shoulder and flung him to the floor. Thinking this would bring Pat out of it, Shelby looked down to see the man curl into the fetal position on the floor.

Seeing he was safe from bullets while lying on the floor, Shelby crawled back over to Ellie who had remained at the window. Ellie was still watching the outside over the sill when Shelby grabbed her ankle. Startled, Ellie yelped and turned and slid down the wall onto her butt. Seeing it was Shelby, she gasped a breath of relief and took the pistol from Shelby.

She now saw for the first time that Pat was a useless mess on the floor of the living room. Motioning and talking to Shelby, she instructed Shelby to crawl back over to Pat and retrieve his service weapon and any extra bullets she could find. Ellie also instructed her to grab the cell phone from her purse on the counter. Watching Shelby go about her new mission, Ellie slowly turned and rose again to look out the window.

She rose to see a man, moving slowly along the bear brush along the river. Raising her pistol, she took aim and fired the gun. Watching the man dive into the brush, Ellie knew it was too great a distance to hit anything with a pistol. Still, Ellie smiled at the thought of the man, diving into the dirt at the sound of the pistol. She had wanted to let the killer know that they had weapons and were not afraid to use them.

Hopefully, the warning shot would keep the killer with his nose in the dirt for a few minutes.

Motioning to Shelby, who was now digging in her purse in the kitchen, Ellie motioned for Shelby to join her in the living room by Pat. Seeing that Pat was still crying and in the fetal position, Ellie knew she had to try and snap the man out of it. Turning his head slightly with her left hand, Ellie raised her right hand and quickly slapped the man across the face with her open hand.

She saw a flicker of recognition in the man's eyes and slapped his face hard again. His whimpering cries stopped at least. He now stared up at Ellie with the look of a man that was now an empty shell. His was spirit broken.

It took considerable effort for Shelby and Ellie to get the big man off the floor and get him moving toward the bedroom. They were just getting him into the bedroom door when another shot burst through the nine-panel window of the front door. Seeing the still open closet doors, Ellie and Shelby threw the man into the closet.

His landing was a bit rough. Ellie hoped the rough landing would bring the man back to reality.

Again, Pat curled into the fetal position. Seeing more blankets on the shelf, Shelby grabbed the remaining blankets and covered the man, lying on the floor. Seeing that he was covered, Shelby slammed the closet doors closed behind her. Since they could not bring him out of it, at least, they would be able to protect him by hiding him. They hoped.

Before leaving the bedroom, Ellie whispered to Shelby to wait for her at the back door. Seeing Shelby off to the back door, Ellie crawled quickly back to the broken window. Ellie again raised her head to look out the window.

A shot fired into the air. Ellie heard the bullet just miss her head. The sound of the bullet made her head spin. Raising her hand with the pistol, Ellie blindly fired out the window at their pursuer. With a ringing in her ears, Ellie again looked out the window. Her eyes just above the window frame.

Seeing the man, Ellie again fired her pistol at him. The cleaner fired back as he dove behind a large boulder at the edge of the yard. Ellie threw herself to the floor a little harder than she anticipated and knocked the wind out of herself in the process. Coughing and gasping on the floor, Ellie looked over to see Shelby was dialing the phone.

Trying to inhale air back into her surprised lungs, Ellie fought with all her might not to cough, and she again looked out the window. Letting off a volley of shots at the boulder, Ellie emptied her weapon at the rock and the man hiding behind it. She may not hit him, but she hoped she would at least scare him. Plus she was angry at the man who did not know her but still wanted to kill her.

Ellie realized her error after discharging her weapon. Now she would have to leave the window and get to her purse for more bullets. As she crawled back over to the counter and retrieved her bag, Ellie heard Shelby, talking to Jim on the phone. Knowing Shelby was doing her best to give directions, Ellie motioned for Shelby to slide the phone over to her at the counter.

It was mistake, sliding the phone. As the phone slid across the floor, it lost the signal strength, and the call was ended. Swearing to herself, Ellie didn't even think of cell reception. She slid the phone back over to Shelby who was now looking very worried.

"Call him back! We lost the signal!" Ellie said as she slid the phone across the floor to Shelby.

Shelby swept the phone up into her hands and was dialing before the phone had even settled into her grip. Reaching Jim back, Shelby heard Ellie say they were on the Dearborn River and to take the Dearborn exit off 15 and head along the gravel road up along the fire hall and follow it back along the river. Shelby quickly repeated the directions to Jim on the line.

Ellie had crawled over to the window by the couch and saw woods at the back of the cabin. It was pretty thick, and she was hoping they could reach the thicket before the gunman reached the cabin. Angry, Ellie stalked from the sofa back over to the broken window. With the spirit of Clint Eastwood, invading her body, Ellie stood along the broken window and peered out. Seeing the rifle barrel still over the boulder, Ellie quickly caught a glimpse of the man behind the rock and began to fire. Standing, she was able to take greater aim and send some bullets, skidding and ricocheting over the top of the boulder, hoping to high heaven that one of the bullets would find its mark.

Hearing the man behind the boulder cuss, Ellie quickly moved over to Shelby and opened the back door. Grabbing her hand, they quickly ran to the safety of the thicket. Finding a well-used deer trail, Ellie followed behind Shelby in the brush. Watching over her shoulder, Ellie hoped this would give them some time before the man realized they were no longer in the cabin.

The two reached a rock face that lead right down to the river. Ellie knew they would have to cross the river and possibly be seen from the house. It was going to be a crap shoot, but they would need to cross and find somewhere to hide until Jim and the other officers showed up.

The water was cool and refreshing as they began to cross. It was Shelby who took the lead and Ellie followed. Seeing Shelby drop into the water with just her face protruding, Ellie followed. Good thing Shelby was along. Ellie had been planning to just walk across the river. This would have left her a sitting duck. The situation quickly reminded Ellie to not let her guard down for a moment.

The current pushed them from the rock face and out into the river. Seeing the shore ahead of them, they pushed their bodies along with the feet and hands. It was a shallow river and didn't give them much leeway in hiding. As quietly as they could muster, both continued to move themselves along the bottom of the river toward the shore. Careful not to splash and give away their position, the shallow water would give little protection against any bullets.

Shelby saw a clump of brush along the shore and motioned to Ellie to follow. Getting to the shore, Shelby didn't want to leave the safety of their hiding place. It was Ellie who got up and got them moving.

In the thicket of river brush, Ellie took Shelby by the hand and led her through the thicket. Finding a small rabbit trail, Ellie got on her knees and began to crawl through the trees. Shelby was going to continue to walk when Ellie whispered that they needed to hide their trail. Ellie hoped that by crawling along this covered rabbit trail that the killer would not think that this may be where they traveled. She hoped it would be them more time.

Ellie hoped that the killer wouldn't follow them just yet, and this rabbit trail would give them just a bit more cover. At least, it would keep them out of the killer's view.

Hearing swearing and yelling from the cabin, both realized their hunter had just found that his prey had slipped away. With a new zeal, both began to crawl quickly along the trail. Coming out to a small meadow that lead into the red pines, Ellie knew that if they headed south, they could follow this until they hit Highway 287. It was going to be a rough walk over the Dearborn Ranch.

Getting to the top of a ridge, overlooking the river and the cabin, Ellie snuck up along some sage brush to get a better look. Looking back down at the cabin, she could see the killer on the back deck clearly searching for them. Ellie looked on as the man headed toward the thicket behind the cabin, hoping they had left no tracks in the dirt of the deer trail.

"We need to keep moving," Shelby whispered.

Nodding in agreement, Ellie and Shelby headed over the ridge just as they heard splashing into the river. The killer had found their trail. It was time to kick it into to high gear. They broke off at a run down the hill away from the lunatic that was hunting them down.

At the bottom of the hill, Shelby stumbled over a log and twisted her ankle badly. Suddenly, Shelby was tumbling head over heels to a screeching stop. Ellie slid to a halt, realizing Shelby was no longer alongside her. Getting Shelby back to her feet, Ellie placed Shelby's arm around her shoulders and tried to steady her. Ellie knew that Shelby was not going to be able to travel far on a twisted ankle. The killer would surely catch up to them pretty quickly. They needed a new plan.

Looking around, Ellie knew they would need a new place to hide and hold up. Shelby was not going to make it very far on that ankle. It was already beginning to swell, and she was limping seriously from the pain. They walked about fifty yards when Ellie was desperately looking for someplace to hide and hold up. Shelby was not going to be able to travel much further. Seeing a rock ledge to the left of them, Ellie led her back down toward the river and the rocks. Getting closer to the rock ledge, it was Shelby who spotted the old lava tube cave first.

These hills are filled with old lava tubes that now make great caves and hiding places, Ellie thought. Moving Shelby as quickly as she could, Ellie kept the duo, traveling as fast as their feet could take them. Shelby was practically running on her ankle. Ellie prayed she wouldn't do any permanent damage but hoped she could keep it up until the safety of the cave.

Reaching the rock face, Ellie realized the cave was about six feet off the ground and didn't know how she was going to get Shelby up onto the ledge. Shelby must have sensed the issue. Moving her arm off Ellie's shoulders, Shelby gripped the rock face in front of her and began to climb. It took all of Ellie's might to push on Shelby's bum and boost her up onto the ledge. It was then that Ellie wondered how the heck she would get up the ledge. It wasn't that high, but there were no places to get a foot hold or grasp with her hands. It was no use.

She decided to turn and run and lead the cleaner away from Shelby. Before Shelby could protest, Ellie was off. She needed to get as far away as possible from Shelby. She couldn't let Shelby be found, or she would most certainly be killed.

Ellie had stopped briefly by the shade of a large pine. She needed to get her bearings and figure out where she was at. Just as she was catching her breath, the dirt exploded at her feet. The gunshot had just missed her leg. Looking behind her, Ellie saw the killer, running to catch up to her. He was shooting as he was running, and this was the only reason Ellie was still alive. The shots, from the man's movements, were wild and off their intended mark.

Her body was moving before her mind was. She was racing toward the river and the safety of the cabin. Ellie looked down toward the river and saw an area that was covered with brush. This would give her some cover. The hillside she now ran down left her a sitting duck. Until she reached the safety of the brush, Ellie knew she was an easy target.

*****

The cleaner was angry with himself. He had been overzealous to shoot at the woman and had missed. He chided himself for not stopping and taking the extra moment to shoot. If he had just done that, then he would be able to look for the other girl.

Instead, he was having to chase the woman and stop her before she reached the cabin. The cleaner knew that he was letting his anger get to him. Anger would only bring mistakes. As he chased the woman, the cleaner began to clear his mind. He needed to focus if he was going to be successful in his kill.

Now the cleaner's mind was clear. He could focus on his job, get it done, and get the hell out of here. His mind now clear. He focused on the job and the kill.

*****

Ellie reached the safety of the thick brush along the river. She plowed through the brush like a bull elk. Branches and leaves tearing at her clothes and her skin. Ellie didn't feel a thing. Adrenaline had taken over.

Suddenly, Ellie exited the brush. Not expecting the water of the river to be so close, she tried to stop, but the forward momentum from her run had propelled her forward, hitting the water with a loud splash! Ellie's feet slipped on the wet rocks! Her feet were coming out from under her. Ellie's body slapped against the water in a belly flop motion.

The water was moving too quickly as Ellie fell. She was in an area of rocky rapids of the river. As Ellie fell into the river, her head slapped down into the river with a thud. Sinking in the water, a slimy rock connected with her head instantly knocking her out cold. Her limp prone limbs bobbed in the cool water as her unconscious body began to float with the current.

Little did she know, but Ellie's clumsiness had just saved her life.

CHAPTER TWENTY-ONE

Jim raced with the other officers to the Dearborn Exit. Praying that he wouldn't get there too late, the gravel road that led back into the Dearborn area was rough and filled with potholes. The police vehicle Jim was driving took a beating.

His fingers and knuckles gripped the wheel. Barely managing to keep his body from leaving the driver's seat, Jim knew he needed to slow down, or he wasn't going to get there at all. A few more good bumps, and Jim was going to lose a tire or the front end.

CHAPTER TWENTY-TWO

Ellie awoke and found herself still in the river. Opening her eyes slowly, the sun directly in her eyes, she tried to move her body and get her bearings. Ellie knew she was pinned. Letting her eyes adjust to the light, she began to look around her.

Confusion filled her mind. How did she get here and where was she?

The last thing Ellie remembered was going through the brush and not being able to stop when she came to the water's edge. She remembered falling into the river. After that, her mind was drawing a blank. Everything had gone black.

She realized that she must have hit her head on one of the rocks and ended up floating under this brush pile. Moving her hand to her head, Ellie felt around for any cuts or bruises. She didn't find a bruise, but she did find one heck of a goose egg at the top of her forehead. The area had swollen to the size of a small chicken egg.

Slowly, she began getting more of her bearings back. Ellie remembered that she was being chased by a killer. Fear suddenly gripped her body. He was still out there somewhere, trying to find her. Her skin was filled with goosebumps, and now, she was suddenly much colder.

Looking around, Ellie could see that she was completely covered by the wood and brush that covered her. Somehow after being knocked out, her body must have floated with the current and been lodged up underneath the pile of dead wood. Realizing how lucky she was to not have drowned, Ellie realized now that she needed to get her body free.

Ellie's right ankle was stuck between two logs at the bottom of the brush pile in the river. Her shoe was holding her foot between the logs. To reach her shoe, she would have to hold her breath and bend her body underwater to reach her shoelaces to untie them.

Taking a deep breath, Ellie submerged her head and bent forward to begin getting her foot free. Getting the wet knot finally undone, Ellie brought her head up out of the water to gasp some air. Her next go around would be to loosen her laces.

Inhaling again to get some fresh air into her lungs, Ellie plunged back under the water to finish the job. Loosening the laces on the shoe, Ellie sat up out of the water. Her head just rising above the surface.

She pulled her foot free from the logs with all her might. The skin of her ankle was tearing on a branch of the submerged log. With this, Ellie let out a scream. The pain raced through her body. Pulling her leg free, she pulled her knees up to her chest. Grasping her ankle with her hand, Ellie could see the blood form in the water.

Looking down, she inspected her ankle to see the extent of the damage. Seeing that the cut was not very deep, the water would help stop the bleeding. She would have a nice size scare on her ankle, but she would live. She might not ever be able to wear pumps and strapless shoes again, but at least, it was only going to be a scar. Thank God, she hadn't ripped off her foot when she pulled her foot free. It had felt like she had left her foot there between the two logs and had come up with just her leg minus the foot.

Ellie was looking over the cut when the wood above her head exploded into a million splinters. Suddenly, her body was being pummeled with a thousand tiny toothpicks. Instantly, Ellie had pulled into a ball to protect herself. It was then she heard his voice.

"Did you like that? You can either come out, or I can keep shooting this pile of logs until I finally reach you!"

Ellie knew it was the voice of the cleaner. Staying silent, Ellie did not know what to say. Her heart was beating very fast as her body raced with adrenaline.

Another close explosion filled Ellie's ears as more wood exploded around her. Ellie knew she had nowhere to go. She knew this would be how she died. Underneath a log and brush pile in cold water of the Dearborn River, no one would know to look under here. She could see that her body would probably not be found until spring when the flood water washed away the debris and her decomposing body was washed away along with the wooden debris.

"Not going to come out? Fine. This is like shooting fish in a barrel. I can sit here all day. How long do you think you can stay soaked and cold in that water?" the cleaner spoke.

It was then that Ellie realized that the man knew she was under the pile but didn't know exactly where. Her silence was keeping her alive a little longer. Ellie tried to remember where the explosions from the gunshots had hit. They were all around her, and none were directly over her. Ellie began to pray that if she stayed under there long enough that someone would hear the gunshots.

Quietly, Ellie recited the *Lord's Prayer*. It gave her comfort to know that someone was watching out for her. She also said a few words to John in prayer. She asked him to put in a good word with God and to look out for her. The prayer gave her a moment of comfort and peace.

Suddenly, another explosion of gunfire filled the air. However, this time, no wood above her head exploded. Ellie slowly looked up at the wood above her wondered what was going on. The last shot had sounded like it came from further away.

Ellie kept looking around. Trying to catch a glimpse of any movement, she was looking up when Ellie felt something warm drop down onto her forehead. Her hand wiped the warm liquid away. Bringing her hand back down, Ellie could see that her hand was covered in blood. Ellie's first thought was that it was her own blood and that she may have hit her head when avoiding the volley of splinters.

Then another drop of blood fell on her cheek. Quickly, she knew that it was someone else's blood. There was a body bleeding on her from on top of the pile. Instantly, Ellie thought of Shelby. Her mind raced. Ellie could keep silent no longer.

"*Shelby!*" Ellie yelled with all her might. Fear filled the air around her.

"Ellie? Where are you?" A distant voice filled Ellie's ears.

"Shelby?" Ellie yelled in the form of a question.

"It's Jim. Ellie? Where are you?"

"Over here, Jim. Thank God! I am under this pile of wood in the river." Relief overwhelmed Ellie.

Ellie heard the splashing of water as tears filled her eyes. She was safe, and they had found her.

A familiar voice brought Ellie out of her thoughts.

"Ellie? Where are you?"

"Shelby? Is that you?" Ellie cried.

"I am here. Sorry it took me so long. It was little hard, crawling all the way down that hill," Shelby said with laughter in her voice.

"Thank God you're okay!" Ellie said.

"I am good. My ankle is a little sore, but I will be fine. By the way, how did you get in there? Are you okay?" Shelby suddenly realized that Ellie was not coming out for some reason.

"I am fine. I think. I got knocked out in the water and floated up under here. Now I can't get out. I think you're going to have to get help to dig me out."

"Ellie, it's Jim. We are here and just hang on. We are going to get you out of there as soon as we can," Jim's words were music to Ellie's ears.

"No hurry. I am okay for now," Ellie said with laughter. "On second thought, could you hurry? This water is kind of cold after you have been in it awhile."

Ellie could hear wood and brush being removed from the pile. Quietly, Ellie said a quick prayer of thanks to God and her husband for looking out for her. She knew her guardian angel husband must have put in a good word for her with God. Ellie smiled to herself.

Ellie opened her eyes to see more sunlight and Shelby and Jim's faces. A smile spread across her lips. She had never been so happy to see two people in her life. It felt so good to feel the warmth of the sun, hitting her face. The heat was such a comfort after the coolness of the water.

Ellie was lost in the warmth of the sun when she realized that she was being pulled by many different pairs of hands, pulling her free of the debris pile. Ellie told them to set her down and that she would walk across the river. Shelby, Jim, and the deputies wouldn't even begin to hear of it. Together, they carried her to the cabin side of the river and sat her down on the bank.

Ellie soaked up the sun and again thanked her lucky stars that she was alive. Looking around at her rescuers, Ellie knew what happiness and the thrill of being alive was all about. These faces that now looked back at her would be forever etched in her memory. The warmth of a happy spirit filled her body. Ellie no longer felt the cold wet feeling of having been in the river.

They were safe.

THREE MONTHS LATER

The months went by slowly as Shelby and Ellie began to heal from their ordeal. The cuts and scrapes would heal, but the emotional scars would take months or years to mend.

The ordeal firmed up in Ellie's mind that she had chosen the right profession. It had solidified her life where at one time, Ellie had no solid ground beneath her feet. This new career gave her life meaning again.

Ellie sat back and thought about the cast of characters that had played such a life-changing part in her existence as a person and as a woman.

SHELBY WALLACE

Shelby will still be healing for many years. While the physical scars have healed. It was the emotional ones that she now carried that worried Ellie the most. It had been very hard on Shelby to sit through the trial and watch the people that were supposed to have loved her, her step father, who had put out a hit on his own daughter, and Shelby's mother, who sat by and did nothing. These emotional scars will probably stay with Shelby for the rest of her life.

Shelby remained strong through the trial. She would not let her parents see her cry. It was only once she was outside the courtroom and away from prying eyes that Shelby was able to let go of some the emotions that were bottled within her. Ellie was most relieved when seeing Shelby breakdown and let go of the anger and pent-up emotions. Ellie had come to love and care about the girl. Ellie knew what it was like to hold on to negative emotions, and she prayed that Shelby would not do the same.

After the trial, Ellie took Shelby under her wing. The girl no longer had a family that loved her. It would be Ellie that would fill this void and become her new family. Shelby soon moved into the house with Ellie. For Ellie, it was wonderful to have company. And for Shelby, it was great to have someone around who loved and cared about her. Ellie also surprised Shelby with a job at her detective agency. For now, Shelby would be maintaining the office, answering phones, and whatever else needed to be done. It gave Shelby an outlet to get outside herself and do something constructive. It also fulfilled the nurturing role of a mother whose other children had left the safety of the nest of home. Ellie was tickled pink.

Ellie encouraged Shelby to enroll in one of the local colleges and take some classes. Shelby surprised Ellie with one better. Shelby let Ellie know one day while in the office that she had enrolled herself in the same school where Ellie became a private detective. Ellie was so touched that she cried and held Shelby for many minutes that day in the office. It made Ellie chuckle now because she found herself becoming a sentimental old fool when it came to the girl. Ellie no longer looked at Shelby as just an employee or previous client. Ellie looked at Shelby as family and as a second daughter.

It was a time that both women needed. Together, they healed from the past and began to look to a future filled with promise. Ellie also began to hope that Shelby may just want to go into business together.

JANET AND JOHN MOORE JR.

Both of Ellie's children were a little less than thrilled when they heard the news of what happened on the Wallace case. However, they had also never seen their mother Ellie so happy. They both decided that they would continue to support and watch over their mother. It also thrilled them to have Shelby living in their family home with their mother. While they would never tell Ellie this, it settled their nerves and fears over their mother. It was nice to have someone they now trusted to be living there and looking after their mother. They knew that it was both women needed in their lives. They had each other to hold on to and heal from the case together.

Both Janet and John had gotten to witness the transformation of the two women together. Somehow, Ellie and Shelby needed one another. They began to heal from each other's experiences. When they heard the news of Shelby going to the private detective school, Janet and John were so happy that they decided to secretly cover all of Shelby's tuition costs. It thrilled them to know that Shelby was working with their mother. Both of them knew that their mother was completely capable, but it still settled any residual fears that popped up over their mother's new profession.

Ellie knew her children's plans and said nothing to them of her knowing. She smiled and relished in the fact that she had two of the best children a mother could have. Ellie felt blessed. It was their love and devotion that guided their actions, and Ellie knew she could never fault them for that.

SUE AND CHUCK

It would still take many months of recovery for Chuck to heal from his wounds. Sue had stepped up like a trooper and became nursemaid. While Sue fretted over Chuck's every move. Ellie laughed because she knew that Sue loved every minute of it. The whole experience had brought them closer together and made their relationship stronger than ever.

Chuck's injuries entailed: two broken ribs, a fractured jaw, major bruising around the liver, two swollen eyes, and many more minor cuts. All in all, his progress would be a full recovery. This news brought tears of joy to Ellie's eyes. Chuck spent a week in the hospital, and Ellie made sure to visit every day. Sue and Chuck had been dragged into the whole affair, and Ellie felt responsible for their troubles. Ellie fussed over Chuck almost as much as Sue did. If the doctors would have been able to fix and heal Chuck, then their love certainly would have.

Sue and Chuck never held any negative feelings toward Ellie. Truth be told, they had rather enjoyed the adventure when looking back at everything. Chuck could have gone without the injuries, but it was worth it to save Shelby's life.

Plus how could they fault Ellie when the whole of the events had made their relationship so much stronger and for the better? In many ways, it was their saving grace. Sue and Chuck now looked to each other with a newfound respect that had only been further strengthened by their love.

OFFICER JIM BARKLEY AND DAUGHTER, MELISSA

Jim was changed by the whole event. He had come across with a new respect for the law and helping others and loving your family. While he loved his family a great deal. The event made him realize just how short life can be. Jim made it a priority to balance work and family life. He would never look back on his life one day and realize that he could have done more. He vowed he would spend as much time as possible with his family. He also knew he would never forget to tell his family just how much he love them. Every day.

Jim got an accommodation for his role in the rescue of his daughter, Ellie, and Shelby. Jim had been forced to make some tough choices after his daughter was kidnapped. He never broke the law and did what was needed to be done to save his daughter. After all, what father wouldn't do the same thing if placed that position?

HOWARD, STEVE, AND THE CLEANER

Howard's body was never found since the cleaner was shot and killed by Officer Barkley out at the cabin on the Dearborn River. Howard's ranch was searched from top to bottom before it was sold at auction. Nothing was ever found. The local sheriff brought cadaver dogs to the ranch to search for other possible bodies. Nothing else was found.

The remaining two, Steve and the cleaner, were buried in the local Helena cemetery. Their funerals were held with little fanfare. The only people attending were the local priest, Ellie, two graveyard attendants, and the two drivers from the funeral home. Their burials were held together, and the two were placed side by side.

Ellie thought it a fitting end for the two to spend eternity together.

Ellie went to the funeral for closure and out of respect for human life. While the two men being buried showed no respect for life. Ellie still felt it necessary to attend. Ellie did not weep. She prayed to God to look after these two lost souls. She really knew of nothing else she could do for them.

Just before the end of the funeral service, Ellie turned and walked away. There was nothing here for her anymore. As Ellie got into her car. She turned one last time to look as the two caskets were being lowered into the ground. It gave her a sense of relief to know the two would never hurt anyone again, but it also left her with a profound sadness at the two men's wasted life.

BILL WALLACE

Bill Wallace was sentenced to two consecutive terms of life in prison. This had suited Shelby just fine. She wanted the man, who would have had her dead, to spend the rest of his life in prison. It was going to be a long time for him to sit and think over his crimes and the lives he had ruined. Shelby was more hurt than angry over all the trial business. She thought it would do Bill some good to sit in prison and have to realize every day why he was there and what he had done.

Bill Wallace never took the stand in his own defense. He never spoke at all during the trial. He had sat at the table with his lawyers, his head down and his eyes vacant. It was the sign of a man that had been broken by the events of his life.

After Mr. Wallace's final sentencing, it was only then that there was a moment of recognition from the man. Before being led from the courtroom by the officers, he turned to Shelby and mouthed the words "I'm sorry."

SHELBY'S MOTHER

Shortly after Bill Wallace was arrested, Mrs. Wallace took her own life. She parked their car in the garage and closed the door and let the engine run. There was no note. No explanation.

EPILOGUE

Ellie's business was now thriving. After the trial coverage and saving Shelby's life, Ellie became somewhat of a local hero. This tickled and confused Ellie. She had been tickled by the attention and increase in her new business but confused at the adulation of the community.

Ellie felt herself just a common person who simply did what needed to be done. That was what made Ellie Lynn Moore so special. She had that common valor.

Ellie was ready to move on from the case and looked forward to the future. She wondered what the next case might bring.

It didn't take long for Ellie to find out just what that next case would be. It would take her across the country and into the wilds of the Upper Peninsula of Michigan.

About the Author

S ava Mathou fell in love with suspense and mystery as a child in Upper Michigan. Sava would lose himself for hours in the books of his school library. (Go, Nordics!)

Sava's love of nature and the outdoors would bring him to the Rocky Mountains of Montana. The long winters provide time to tinker with his writing and explore and develop characters.

Sava grew up surrounded by strong women (friends, sisters, aunts, and Mom). Sava tries to bring that strength and awesomeness through in his books' characters.